About Joss Wood

Joss Wood wrote her first book at the age of eight and has never really stopped. Her passion for putting letters on a blank screen is matched only by her love of books and travelling—especially to the wild places of Southern Africa—and possibly by her hatred of ironing and making school lunches.

Fuelled by coffee, when she's not writing or being a hands-on mum, Joss—with her background in business and marketing—works for a non-profit organisation to promote the local economic development and collective business interests of the area where she resides. Happily and chaotically surrounded by books, family and friends, she lives in Kwa-Zulu Natal, South Africa, with her husband, children and their many pets.

TM

It was Only a Kiss

Joss Wood

First published in Great Britain 2013
by Mills & Boon, an imprint of Harlequin (UK) Limited.
Harlequin (UK) Limited, Eton House, 18-24 Paradise Road,
Richmond, Surrey TW9 1SR

© Joss Wood 2013

ISBN: 978 0 263 23478 7

Harlequin (UK) policy is to use papers that are natural, renewable and recyclable products and made from wood grown in sustainable forests. The logging and manufacturing process conform to the legal environmental regulations of the country of origin.

Printed and bound in Great Britain
by CPI Antony Rowe, Chippenham, Wiltshire

Also by Joss Wood

Wild About the Man
She's So Over Him

Did you know these are also available as eBooks?
Visit www.millsandboon.co.uk

For my children, Rourke and Tess,
who are all things bright and beautiful.

PROLOGUE

Eight years ago...

'So, IN CONCLUSION, I think the marketing strategy your people presented to you is hackneyed, stupid and asinine, and pays absolutely no attention to your demographics, to the market research or to where your competitors are placing themselves. It's under-researched and knocked together, and if you follow it I guarantee that you will lose most of your market share in five years' time—if not your business.'

Luke Savage looked across his messy desk at the earnest young woman perched on the edge of her chair, her face animated with youthful zeal and a healthy dose of arrogance. What was her name again? He glanced down at the file in front of him. Jess Sherwood. She was twenty-two, he read, and was currently doing her MBA in Marketing. The file did state that she was over-blessed with brains—her school and university achievements were, to put it mildly, impressive—but it failed to mention that she was solidly gorgeous as well.

A true brown-eyed blonde.

She was quite a parcel and, boy, did she know it.

Luke kept his face impassive as she draped one long, slim leg over the other and lightly linked her hands around a bare knee, an index finger tapping away. She wore a short, flouncy dress, falling off one shoulder and showing a thin purple bra strap, and belted at slim hips by a broad leather belt. Falling to mid-thigh, it was too short, too casual, and too sexy an outfit for work—but she wore it with careless confidence.

Luke, who was seldom surprised at much, was taken aback by her self-importance and her balls-to-the-wall chutzpah. She'd been placed as an intern for the summer holidays, to gain work experience within St Sylve's marketing depart-ment—*his* marketing department, since he'd recently inher-ited the generations-old family vineyard. She'd ambushed him as he'd been about to leave, barged into his office and said that she felt 'morally obligated'—he curled his lip at the phrase—to tell him that his decisions sucked and his mar-keting plan was dreadful. And now she had the temerity to predict the failure of his business.

Her mobile rang and Luke hissed his annoyance as she dived for her bag and pulled out the phone, squinting at the display. She flashed him a wide smile that was charming but devoid of apology. 'Sorry—I have to take this.'

Whatever—I'm just your boss. Why don't I just wait while you finish arranging your social life?

He felt twenty years older than her, rather than six, and he probably was in experience. University was a dim and distant memory, clouded by the fourteen- to sixteen-hour days he'd been working for the past seven years.

Lately he'd felt perpetually exhausted, but if he'd had the energy he'd have got up and yanked her mobile from her ear and torn her a new one. Which he intended to do when she finished cooing into her mobile.

Her words rattled around his brain… *You will lose most of your market…*

Hell, he was losing St Sylve. It was failing… Not his fault or his failure, because failure wasn't what he did—well, it wasn't what he'd been allowed to do. Sport? He'd excelled at most. Academics? Scholarships and huge job offers had translated into his being able to set up his own company three years ago...one of the youngest venture capitalists in the country. Marriage? Okay, he'd dropped the ball on that one, but in a couple of weeks the divorce would be through and he'd be rid of the credit-card-digesting monster he'd married.

Now, if he could get this other creature out of his office without strangling her, he'd consider himself a saint.

Jess snapped her mobile closed, slipped it back into her bag and looked at him expectantly. Stuck-up, arrogant little witch.

Sexy, though....

Luke's boots dropped from the corner of his desk to the floor and he stood up slowly, knowing that his face displayed none of his anger. As a child, living with his volatile, demanding father—his mother had died when he was three—he'd learnt early that showing emotion of any sort could be used against him, so he'd perfected his stoic mask.

He watched her through half-closed lids. She looked relaxed, leaning back in the chair, a small smile edging the corners of her very sexy mouth upwards. Give her a couple of years and she'd be hell on wheels...if she could keep her cocky opinions to herself.

'Interesting perspective,' Luke said mildly. He saw her mouth open to speak and lifted a finger to silence her. 'If I cared.'

Mouth open but no words emerging...it was a start, Luke thought. Placing his hands on his desk, he leaned forward with a gesture that was meant to be intimidating and finally allowed her to see his fury. He felt marginally appeased when her eyes widened and she bit her bottom lip.

'You arrogant, snotty child!' He deliberately kept his voice even, knowing that harsh words delivered coldly had more of an effect than ranting and raving. 'How dare you walk into my company and my office and presume to tell me what to do with my business and how to do it? Who the *hell* do you think you are?' he suddenly roared, and Jess winced as his words bounced off the walls.

Jess lifted up her hands and he noticed that she didn't look particularly scared. Hell, she didn't look scared, period.

'You don't understand—'

'What I understand is that you are a bright young thing who has always been told that she's wonderful—clever and bright and talented. Pretty too. After so much unstinting admiration and affirmation, how could you think I wouldn't want to hear the pearls of wisdom that fall so effortlessly from your lips?'

Jess jumped to her feet. 'Luke, I—'

'It's Mr Savage to you! I'm your boss, not your friend! If you want to get anywhere you'd better bloody learn some humility and some respect! I have my own MBA, sunshine, and I've run a successful company for years. I have put in the sweat and tears and the work to earn the right to have an opinion. You haven't!'

'Stop yelling at me!'

Luke looked at her and shook his head. A part of him—okay, all his boy bits—thought she looked magnificent, with her heaving chest and wild eyes, fury staining her high cheekbones like the rasp of a lover's beard. She looked furious, but not intimidated, and a part of him had to admire her courage.

A very small part of him.

'It's not my fault your marketing plan sucks! I'm just telling you that the St Sylve vineyard will suffer if you do not adjust your strategy!'

'Because you say so?'

'Yes! Because I'm damn good at this. I just know it won't work!'

Luke rubbed a hand over his chin. 'So, now you have a crystal ball as well? Can you tell me if I'm going to get skinned in my divorce or whether the price of oil will drop?'

'Of course you will get skinned—that's what happens when you marry a gold-digger! And, no, the oil price is going to keep climbing. The markets are too unstable at the moment to allow a drop,' Jess replied.

Luke could not believe that she hadn't picked up his sarcasm. 'For someone who's only been here a couple of months, you seem to be firmly plugged in to vineyard gossip.'

Jess sent him a cheeky grin. 'Thank you.'

'It wasn't a compliment.'

'I know.'

He was going to kill her. Luke stalked around the desk and gripped her slim shoulders with his much bigger hands. 'I'm not sure whether to strangle you or smack you.'

Jess tossed her head of honey-coloured curls and looked up at him with bold and defiant brown eyes. A brown so deep it could almost be black.

'You're not the type to hit a woman.' Jess lifted one shoulder and sent him a look that was as powerful as it was ageless. 'And you're just annoyed because you know I'm right.'

'Annoyed? I'm way past annoyed and on my way to incandescently livid.'

Under his hands Jess lifted her shoulders. 'But why? I'm just telling the truth.'

He was exasperated at her cheek, but he was even more furious because she had his blood pressure spiking and his pants jumping.

'You are cheeky, conceited, smug and vain,' Luke muttered as his lips edged their way down to hers. He could see the challenge in those eyes that held his...and as well as not tolerating failure, he also never backed away from a challenge.

Jess tipped her chin up and he could feel her breath on his lips. She felt slight and feminine in his arms, and while he knew that he was playing with fire he couldn't let her go.

'Then why are you going to kiss me?'

'Because it's either that or put you over my knee,' Luke growled.

'But you don't like me,' Jess stated.

'God, how old are you? Attraction has nothing to do with liking someone.'

'It should.'

'You're naïve.'

'Kissing me would be a mistake,' Jess whispered even as her lips lifted to his.

'Too damn late.'

Electricity arced and thunder rolled as he yanked her slim frame into his solid chest, burrowing his hands into her hair to move her head so that he could deepen the angle of the kiss, could touch every corner of her sexy mouth with his tongue. His hand dropped to her lower back and he pulled her against him. His stomach swooped when he felt her hips against his, her small hands sneaking under his shirt to feel the skin of his back and shoulders.

He'd never been this hot this quickly for anyone. Luke closed his eyes as her quick tongue tasted his bottom lip, then tangled with his in a long, lazy slide. One hand held the back of her head and the other skimmed the side of her torso, its thumb sliding over the swell of her—

This had gone too far, Luke told himself. He had to stop this. Now.

Instead he ran the palms of his hands up the back of her silky-soft thighs and gripped her butt.

Holy hell, he thought as his hands encountered nothing but warm skin. Where were her panties…? Their kiss deepened and went from crazy to wild. He massaged her as he pulled her up against him and…oh, there it was. An ultra-thin strand of cotton. He traced his fingers upward and found the T of her thong, embellished with what seemed to be a fabric heart flat against her lower back. Luke hooked his thumb under the T and rubbed that gorgeous patch of skin. So soft, so smooth... He could snap the cord with a quick twist...

Luke wrenched himself away from her, sucked in a breath and hoped that she didn't notice him gripping the edge of the desk for balance. She looked glorious, with her flashing eyes, swollen mouth and mussed hair. He could take her right now, right here in the late-afternoon sun.

It shook him how much he wanted to see her naked, sprawled across his desk, her body exposed to his hot gaze, her creamy skin flushed with pleasure.

Luke summoned up the last reserves of his self-control and slowly felt his self-restraint returning. When he felt his big brain had the edge over his little one, he stood up straight and wordlessly pointed to the door.

Jess nodded as she straightened her shirt. 'Right—time for me to leave.' She rocked on her heels, then dug in her tote bag and pulled out a large envelope which she placed on his desk. 'A marketing strategy—an alternative to what you have now. Maybe we can discuss it another time?'

Un-frickin'-believable.

Had she heard anything he'd said before he'd kissed the hell out of her? Obviously not.

Luke shook his head. 'I don't think so.'

A tiny frown appeared between her arched brows. 'Why not?'

Luke walked around his desk and flopped into his chair. 'Because you're fired. Pack up your stuff and get off my property. Immediately.'

CHAPTER ONE

Jessica
I seem to be missing one of my Shun knives. A boning
and filleting knife. If you do not return it I'll be forced
to ask you to replace it as I bought it during our trip
to the States. They retail for around 200 US dollars.
Grant

Jess Sherwood dropped her head as the e-mail on her screen winged its way to the deleted folder. Grant was smoking something very green and very strong if he thought that she had any intention of paying him another cent. Who had supported him and his extravagant lifestyle when he'd lost his job and while he'd struggled to get his fledgling catering business off the ground?

And, while she'd dished out the money and the sympathy, every day when she'd left for work he'd found something else to do. Or perhaps she should say *someone* else to do... the blonde living in the simplex opposite them.

Jerk.

The door to her office opened and Jess watched Ally enter, her iPad in her hand. Jess counted her blessings that her stunningly efficient office manager was also her best and most trusted friend.

'What's the matter?' Ally asked, dropping into the chair opposite Jess.

Jess waved at her computer. 'Grant. Again. Looking for something called a Shun knife. Um…what's a Shun knife?'

Ally, well acquainted with Jess's lack of culinary skills, smiled. 'It's a brand of expensive kitchen knives. Nice.'

'Well, if I find it in my kitchen it's yours,' Jess said glumly.

'What else is the matter?' Ally placed her iPad on the desk.

Jess waved at her computer. 'Grant's trying to yank my chain.'

Ally's bold red lips quirked. 'Judging by the scowl on your face, I'd say "mission accomplished".'

Jess wrinkled her nose. 'He's the larva that grows on the dung of…'

'Yeah, yeah—heard it all before. It was over months ago, so why are you still so PO-ed?'

Jess rested her elbows on her desk and shoved her fingers into her hair, considering Ally's question. It had been a year since Grant had lost his high-powered job as brand manager for a well-known clothing chain, and six months since she'd caught him in their bed with what's-her-name with the stupid Donald Duck tattoo on her butt…

Since she'd been on top when Jess had walked into the bedroom the image was indelibly printed on her mind.

Okay, so the incident had also catapulted her back to that dreadful period in her teens when— No, she wasn't going to think about that. It was enough to remember that she now knew the pain infidelity caused—first- and second-hand.

She was now wholly convinced that any woman who handed over emotional control to another person in the name of love had to be fiercely brave or terminally nuts.

She was neither.

'Well?' When Jess didn't speak, Ally shook her head. 'We've shared everything from pregnancy scares—yours—

to one-night stands—mine—and everything in between, so talk to me, Jessica Rabbit.'

Jess managed a smile at her old nickname. 'I'm angry, sure, but at myself as well as him. I'm livid that he managed to slip his affair under my radar—that I wasn't astute enough to realise that he was parking his shoes under someone else's bed.'

Ally stood up, walked over to the credenza and shoved two cups under the spout of Jess's beloved coffee machine. After doctoring them both, Ally handed Jess her cup, put her back to the window and perched her bottom on the sill.

'I spoke to Nick on my way to work.' Jess couldn't help the smile that drifted across her face. It was wonderfully good to have an open, relaxed relationship with her brother again, after years of him operating on the periphery of her life. 'He's so damn happy with Clem, and I know that they have something special. The last of my brothers—all of whom sowed enough wild oats to cover Africa—has settled down.'

'And you're wafting in the wind?' Ally placed her hands on the windowsill behind her. 'And that bothers you because it's something your brothers have got right and you haven't. Love is not a contest, Jess. Do you know what your problem is?' Ally continued.

'No, but I'm sure you're going to tell me,' Jess grumbled. She wasn't sure she wanted to hear what she had to say…Ally seldom pulled her punches.

'You raised the topic,' Ally pointed out. 'Do you want me to tell you what you want to hear or the truth?'

'That's a rhetorical question, right?' Jess took a deep breath. 'Okay, I'll take a brave-girl pill…hit me.'

'One sentence: you're so damned scared of being vulnerable that you try to control everything in a relationship.'

Hearing her earlier thought about control so eloquently explained floored Jess. Did her best friend know her or what?

'Being single suits you and not being in love suits you even better.'

'Can I change my mind and ask you to tell me what I want to hear?' Jess protested. She wasn't sure if she wanted to hear any more about her romantic failings.

'To you, being in love means losing control—and to a control freak that is the scariest thing in the world.'

'I am *not* a control freak!' Jess retorted, heat in her voice.

Ally's mouth dropped open. 'You big, fat liar! You are all about control. That's why you choose men you can control.'

'You are so full of it.' Jess sulked.

'You know I'm right,' Ally retorted.

This was the problem with good friends. They knew you better than you knew yourself, Jess grumbled silently. Deciding that Ally was looking far too smug, she decided to change the subject, vowing to give their conversation some more thought later.

Maybe.

If she felt like digging into her own psyche with a hand drill.

Right now they needed to work. She nodded to the iPad and listened and made notes as Ally updated her on the projects she wasn't personally involved with. Jess gave her input and instructions and ran through some office-related queries.

They were concentrating on interpreting some tricky data from a survey when Jess's PA put through a call from Joel Andersen, a much larger competitor whose company owned branches throughout Africa.

He was also one of the few people in the industry she liked and trusted.

Ally started to rise, but Jess shook her head and hit the speaker button. She would tell Ally about the call anyway, so she'd save herself the hassle. She and Joel traded greetings and Jess waited for him to get to the point. Joel, not one to beat around the bush, jumped right in.

'I was wondering…what did you think about Luke Savage's e-mail? I presume you're going to his briefing session for the new marketing strategy he wants to implement for his winery? I thought that if we catch the same flight to Cape Town we could share a car to St Sylve.'

Jess's heart did a quickstep as she tried to keep up with Joel. She sent a glance at her monitor; she most definitely had *not* received an e-mail from Luke Savage…

Not knowing what to think, she decided that the only thing she could do was to pump Joel for information. 'So, what do *you* think?'

'About St Sylve? He needs it… I heard that he commissioned market research with Lew Jones and is open to something new and hip. But with two hundred years of Savage wine-making history and tradition, that could backfire.'

She didn't think so… She hadn't eight years ago and she didn't now. It was about time he looked at updating his marketing, Jess grumbled silently. Over the years she'd kept an eye on the vineyard and was saddened by its obviously diminishing market share. The advertising was dry, the labels boring and its promotion stuffy.

And, since she was the only one who'd ever hear it, she sent Luke Savage a silent I-told-you-so.

Jess widened her eyes at Ally, who was frowning in confusion. 'My PA is just updating my iPad…what time was the briefing again?' she lied.

'Ten-thirty on Friday morning at the estate,' Joel replied.

Bless his heart—he didn't suspect a thing.

'So, shall I have my PA look at flights?'

'Uh…let me come back to you on that. I've been out for a day or two and haven't quite caught up. I have clients in Cape Town to see, so I might fly in earlier,' Jess fudged, and grimaced at Ally, who was now leaning forward, looking concerned.

'Well, let me know,' Joel told her before disconnecting.

Jess scrunched up her face. Damn Luke Savage and his injured pride. Her instinctive reaction was that the St Sylve campaign was hers—it had been hers eight years ago and it was still hers. There was no way she would allow another company to muck it up a second time...

Jess stood and placed her hands on her hips. 'What do you know about St Sylve wines?'

Ally's brown furrowed in thought. 'The vineyard has produced some award-winning wines, but it hasn't translated that into sales.'

It had taken a bit longer than Jess had thought, but her predictions about St Sylve had come true...and she felt sad. This was one of the few occasions when she would have been happy to be wrong...*wished* she was wrong. St Sylve was a Franschoek institution—one of the very few vineyards owned by the same family of French settlers who'd made their home in the valley in the early nineteenth century. She'd loved the three months she'd spent at the vineyard—had been entranced by the buildings, so typical of the architecture of the Cape Colony in the seventeenth and eighteenth centuries, with its whitewashed outer walls decorated with ornate gables and thatched roofs.

Apart from the main residence and guest house, the property still had its original cellar, a slave bell, stables and service buildings.

It also had Luke Savage, current owner, who'd fired her and kicked her off his property after kissing her senseless.

Jess quickly recounted her history with Luke to Ally, who was equally entertained and horrified. 'He *fired* you?'

'I deserved it. At twenty-two I thought I was God's gift to the world,' Jess replied.

Learning that she wasn't had been painful, but necessary. While she hadn't been wrong about the marketing of St Sylve—as she'd suspected, the campaign had been a dismal failure—she'd been arrogant, impulsive and rude, approaching him the way she had.

Jess paced the area in front of her desk. 'As much as I hate to admit it, I owe Luke Savage a debt of gratitude for a major life lesson. I needed my wings clipped and to learn that being first in class, being able to regurgitate facts and figures from a textbook, means diddly-squat in the business world.'

Jess put her hands on her waist and looked at the ceiling. Then she sent Ally a rueful look. 'We had this massive shouting match and then he kissed me. He was a dynamite kisser. A master of the art.' She blew air into her cheeks. 'The best ever.'

'Ooh.' Ally wiggled her bottom.

'I don't even know if I can call what happened between us kissing…it was too over-the-top outrageous to be labelled a simple kiss.'

But then Luke Savage had been anything *but* simple. Jess sighed. He'd been one long, tall slurp of gorgeousness: bold, deep green eyes, chocolate-cake-coloured hair, tanned skin. The list went on… Broad shoulders, slim hips and long, long legs…

'Jess? Hello?'

Jess snapped her head up. 'Sorry—mind wandering.'

'He sounds delicious, but the question is…what are you going to do about St Sylve? Are you going to go to the briefing session?'

'Without an invitation?' Jess looked at the ceiling. 'I'm tempted. I wish I could demand to implement a strategy for him.' Images flashed through her head of possible advertisements. Her creative juices were flowing and she hadn't even seen the brief yet. She *really* wanted to get stuck into dreaming up a new campaign for St Sylve.

But Luke was still the only man who'd ever short-circuited her brain when he kissed her…and if she was being sensible that was a really good reason *not* to work for him. She didn't think she'd be very effective, constantly drooling over her keyboard.

'Phone the guy and ask him!' Ally demanded, and Jess managed a smile.

'Not an option. We didn't get off on the right foot.' Jess held up her hand at Ally's protest.

Why did her stomach feel all fluttery, thinking about him? It had been so long ago…but the thought of seeing him again made her jittery and…*hot*.

She didn't want to get involved. She liked being single. She wanted to play on the edges of the circle and keep it all on the surface.

Why did even the *thought* of Luke feel like a threat to that?

Jess shook her head, utterly bewildered. Where on earth had *that* left-of-centre thought barrelled in from? Sometimes she worried herself, she really did…

Luke Savage sat on one of the shabby couches on the wide veranda of his home, propped his battered boots on an equally battered oak table and heaved a sigh. He lifted his beer bottle to his lips and let the icy liquid slide down his dusty throat.

He opened his eyes and watched as the sun dipped behind the imposing Simonsberg Mountain—one of a couple of peaks that loomed over the farm. As the sun dropped, so did the temperature, so he pulled on his leather-and-wool bomber jacket.

'I take it you saw the monthly financials for St Sylve?' Kendall said eventually.

'We're still not breaking even.' Luke sat up and placed his

forearms on his thighs, let his beer bottle dangle from his fingers. 'I can't keep ploughing money into this vineyard. At some stage it has got to become self-sustaining,' Luke added when his two closest friends said nothing.

Kendall de Villiers shook a head covered in tight black curls. His dark eyes flashed and his normally merry creme-caramel face tightened. 'We know that your father sucked every bit of operating capital out of this business before he died and left you with a massive overdraft and huge loans. You've paid off the lion's share of those loans—'

'With money I made on other deals—not from the vineyard bank accounts,' Luke countered. Kendall knew his businesses inside and out; he was not only his accountant and financial analyst, but a junior partner in his venture capitalist business.

'The wines we produce are good,' Owen Black said in his laid-back way.

Luke wasn't fooled by his dozy, drawling voice. Owen was one of the hardest-working men he'd ever come across. As farm manager, responsible for the vines and the olives, the orchards and the dairy, he got up early and went to bed late. Just as he did.

'You've won some top awards over the last few years, including Wine Maker of the Year,' Owen continued.

'It means nothing if we're not selling the bottles,' Luke retorted. 'Our wines aren't moving—not from the cellar here, and not from the wine shops.'

When both his friends didn't reply, Luke twisted his lips and said what they were obviously thinking. 'Because our marketing strategy sucks. It's boring and old-fashioned and aimed at anyone standing in God's waiting room.' Luke leaned back and popped a cushion behind his head. 'Why didn't I see it before?'

Because a smart-mouthed girl once told me it was so and I was too full of offended pride to listen to her. And because

I had so much else on my plate. I figured I could let it slide for a while... Stupid, stupid, stupid.

The Savage tradition of 'letting the wine speak for itself' was being drowned out by the splashy campaigns and eye-catching labels of their competitors. But Luke hadn't changed it because tradition was everything at St Sylve.

Hadn't his grandfather and father drummed that into him? Excellence and tradition—that was what Savage men strove for, what St Sylve stood for.

He got the reference to excellence, but tradition was killing him. He had to change something and quickly. Of course, he knew that both his father and his grandfather and every other type of forefather he had would do a collective roll in their graves...but if he didn't do something drastic to increase sales he'd either have to sell St Sylve or resign himself to using whatever profits he made on other deals to subsidise the estate. At some point he'd like to have a life, instead of working two full-time jobs.

Kendall had returned to the subject of the marketing strategy and Luke tuned in, idly remembering that somewhere he had a copy of the plan Miss Smarty Pants had tossed onto his desk so many years ago. He wondered what he'd done with it. It would be interesting to see what she had to say...

'Remind me—who is attending?' Luke asked Kendall.

His friend didn't need to consult his computer and quickly ran through the names.

'Not Jess Sherwood Concepts?' Luke asked.

'You specifically told me not to,' Kendall protested.

Luke raised his hand. 'Just checking.'

Kendall narrowed his eyes and shook his head. 'Why, I have no idea. Despite being a young company, Jess Sherwood has had some impressive campaigns over the last couple of years.'

'And you don't want her?' Owen asked Luke, puzzled.

'What's the problem? Why wouldn't you invite her to the briefing session?'

Jess Sherwood. He could still recall her big brown eyes and those honey-blonde curls, that gangly body and smooth, creamy skin. The way she'd tasted…strawberry lip gloss and spearmint gum. He could barely remember what his ex-wife looked like, yet he could remember that Jess had three freckles in a triangular cluster just below her right ear.

He would rather eat nails than approach Jess for a new marketing strategy—as good as she was reputed to be. Call him proud, call him stubborn, but she was a sharp thorn in his memory…the hottest and yet strangest sexual encounter of his life.

And, despite being so young, she'd seen the writing on the wall. With all his degrees and experience, his ability to look into the heart of a business and pinpoint the bottlenecks and constraints, he'd been unable to do it for his own vineyard.

Talk about not being able to see the wood for the trees. Or, in his case, the grapes for the vines.

Owen placed his bottle on the coffee table and frowned. 'What's your beef with Jess Sherwood?'

'Jess interned at St Sylve the summer I inherited this place. I was in the midst of getting divorced from Satan's sister and I didn't want to be here. I didn't want the responsibility of the vineyard, I was working all hours, and I was…'

'Miserable?' Kendall supplied when he hesitated. 'Depressed, angry, shirty, despondent?'

Hell, he'd been entitled to lick his wounds. He'd always wanted to be part of a family, and had thought that Mercia was what he needed to realise that dream. And she'd promised exactly what he'd wanted to hear…family, roots, stability… What was important to him had seemed to be what was important to her. She'd done an excellent job of camouflaging her true agenda until they were hitched, and when he'd woken up three months later he'd found himself legally bound to a freedom-seeking, greedy, money-guzzling shrew. Over the next two years he'd come to the dawning realisation that he'd been well and truly screwed.

Again. And not in a good way. It still burned that he'd been stupid enough to be so comprehensively manipulated.

As a result he'd made the decision never to get involved in a serious relationship or to allow a woman to clean him out financially and emotionally again. While he'd been grateful to see the back of her, watching his lifelong dream of being part of a family fade had stung. A lot.

Luke narrowed his eyes at Kendall. 'Do you want to hear about Jess Sherwood or not?' he demanded. 'She was as gorgeous as all hell and she knew it. Entitled, privileged, unbelievably annoying. I had barely been introduced to her and had only seen her around a time or two. Then she just barged into my office and proceeded to lecture me on my marketing department. She called them a herd of dinosaurs and threw all those marketing terms at my head. Told me what I was doing wrong and how to fix it.'

'So you kicked her off the premises?' Kendall grinned at Luke's nod.

Owen grinned too. 'She sounds like a pistol.'

'Jess Sherwood is such a madam that she'll gloat about being right, rub my face in the fact that St Sylve needs her—I need her. I just don't want to have to cope with her.'

Especially if she's still as sexy as she was. Luke didn't tell them that he'd kissed her stupid and been kissed back.

'So I don't want to deal with her. Big personality clash.'

'It was a long time ago,' Owen pointed out. 'You should at least have asked her to the briefing session to see what she says.'

'No. I can't work with her. So what's the point of her quoting?' Luke stated, knowing that he said it because if she was still anywhere as hot as she'd been when she was younger he'd have a hard time keeping his tongue from hitting the floor every time she walked into the room. His attraction to her memory was still, crazily, *that* strong.

It wasn't like him. He had a calm, satisfying…arrangement with the owner of a wine store in the city. When either of them needed company, or sex, or a date to a function, the other was their 'go-to' person. No fuss, no expectation, no emotion—no imagining wild sex on his office desk in the afternoon sunlight…

Luke leaned forward and sent his friends a serious look. 'Look, this isn't about a business I've picked up and intend to flog. It's about St Sylve—about getting it back to where it was as the premier vineyard in the country. It's hard enough dealing with the situation my father left me, let alone her.'

Over the years he'd tried to distance himself emotionally from the estate and the winery, but he still couldn't manage to treat the multi-generational enterprise he'd inherited like any other arbitrary business.

It was his birthright—both his joy and his burden. His pleasure and his pain. A source of pride and an even bigger source of resentment. He loved and hated it with equal fervour.

'I think you're making a big mistake,' Kendall insisted. 'She's a professional…'

'End of discussion,' Luke said genially, but he made sure that his friends heard the finality in his voice. He valued their opinions, but the decision rested with him. Jess Sherwood was the type of woman who upset apple carts, turned things on their heads, inside out. While he reluctantly accepted that she was probably exactly what St Sylve the business needed, it would be detrimental to *him*, to his calm and ordered life.

Just this once he was putting himself first...surely at thirty-six he was entitled to do that once in a while?

CHAPTER TWO

Jess, with Ally at her side, walked into the tasting room adjoining the St Sylve cellars, looked at the chairs set up in two perfectly aligned rows and sighed in relief when she didn't see Luke Savage. Kendall De Villers, Luke's right-hand man, looked very surprised when she introduced herself, and she saw a momentary flash of panic flick over his face before he smiled slowly.

'Well, this is going to be interesting,' he told her, with a wicked glint in his fantastic brown-black eyes.

'Did he honestly think I wouldn't hear about this or doesn't he care?' Jess bluntly asked.

'Uh…'

Jess waved her question away. 'Anywhere I can hide where he won't see me? At least until he's finished the briefing?'

Kendall lifted his eyebrows. 'In that outfit? Not a chance in hell.'

Jess didn't bother to look down. She was wearing a black, body-hugging wraparound dress, black suede heels that made her calves look fabulous and a long string of fake pearls. With her bright blonde hair and bold lipstick, she was as inconspicuous as a house on fire.

'Where is he?' Jess asked, looking around the room.

'Probably doing something farmy…' Kendall pushed back

the sleeve on his immaculately tailored suit and glanced at his watch. 'Take a seat. We should be starting soon.'

'Rescue me if it looks like he's about to kill me?' she asked, only half joking.

Kendall grinned. 'I'm not that brave. Sorry, sister, but you're on your own.'

Jess took her seat next to the wall of the cellar, behind the broad shoulders of the creative director of Cooper & Co, and hoped Luke wouldn't recognise her.

She leaned her shoulder into Ally's and spoke in a low voice. 'Have I lost my marbles?'

'It's a question that keeps me awake at night,' Ally responded. 'Why?'

'We're across the country, in a briefing session we haven't been invited to, to listen to a briefing by a man who, I suspect, doesn't forgive and doesn't forget.'

What was she thinking?

'Mmm, if one of your staff did this you'd drop-kick them off a cliff.'

She loved Ally, but frequently wished she could be a little less honest, not quite so forthright.

'Why are we here, then?'

'Because this is still my campaign!' Jess hissed. It had been her campaign eight years ago and nobody else was going to get their grubby little hands on it.

She just had one little problem: convincing Luke to see it her way.

And there he was, striding in from a side door to the podium, tucking his cap into the back pocket of his jeans. Such an attractive man, she thought, in a hunter-green long-sleeved T-shirt that skimmed his broad shoulders and wide chest and fell untucked over the waist of over-laundered faded jeans. His dark brown hair brushed his collar and fell in shaggy waves over his ears; he desperately needed a haircut, and he could do with a shave… There was designer stubble and there was three-day-old beard.

And then there was that spectacular butt, hugged by the thin fabric of his jeans as he turned his back on his audience to talk to Kendall. Jess caught Kendall's wince at his lack of formal attire and thought that only Luke would walk into a room full of Italian suits and designer ties in his farm clothes and not give a damn. Jess leaned forward. Was that a greasy palm print on the pocket of his jeans? Then Luke crouched to tie the lace in his boot and his shirt rode up his back. She could see the line between his tanned back and his white hips above the soft leather belt. Jess swallowed the saliva that pooled in her mouth and wondered how warm that strip of skin would feel, how it would taste…

Ally let out a low whistle. 'Oh, my giddy aunt.'

'Gorgeous, isn't he?' Jess asked. This would be so much easier if he'd picked up a beer gut, lost his hair…

'Not him! Well, he is—but the redhead! I wouldn't mind it if he parked his shoes under my bed!' Ally muttered back, waving her hand in front of her face. 'Yum!'

He did have attractive friends, Jess admitted, but for her they were missing that X factor. The one that screamed power and control and sheer masculine presence. Some would say it was testosterone, some supreme self-confidence, but it was more than that. Whatever the mystery ingredient that made Luke more of a man, he'd been given an overdose of it at birth…

It was a good thing she was sitting down because seeing him, so tall and strong, cut her legs out from under her. He was all chemistry and potency and lust and pheromones and… Why was he still the only man she'd ever met who had the ability to vacuum every thought from her brain? Who was able to send her blood to pool in her womb, flush her face and body with pleasure, with nothing more than a look from those fabulous eyes?

Good grief, she thought as their eyes connected and held, if he kept looking at her like that—with barely concealed heat and open hostility—she would dissolve into a puddle on the floor.

Hot, hot, *hot*.

'He's clocked you,' Ally told her, very unnecessarily.

'Yeah, I noticed.'

'You're in trouble,' Ally sang, *sotto voce*. 'He looks like he wants to gobble you up in one big bite.'

Jess kicked her ankle to get her to shut up.

'If I'm really, really lucky,' Jess countered as those green eyes swept over her again, 'he'll just ignore me.'

She heard Ally's sarcastic snort. 'And maybe pigs will grow glittery fairy wings and fly.'

'You could, at the very least, have changed into a clean pair of pants!' Kendall muttered, looking exceptionally irritated.

'I intended to but I ran out of time,' Luke countered, jamming his hands into his pockets. On good days he never had time to spare, and even in July, the heart of winter in the Cape, there was work to be done. He and Owen were overseeing the pruning of the vines, and in the winery the wines needed to be analysed for pH, acidity, alcohol content and a handful of other tests that needed to be done.

'If you'd let me hand this marketing stuff over to you then you wouldn't have to nag me about my clothes. And you can nag for Africa, Ken.'

'Get stuffed,' Kendall retorted. 'And they want to see the Savage of St Sylve.'

'This isn't an estate in England! The Savage of St Sylve, my ass!' Luke grumbled.

'It's as close as it gets. Now, will you please get on with it?'

Kendall nodded to the podium and Luke sighed. The Savage of St Sylve? Today he would happily be anyone else, he thought as he turned to face his audience. His gaze skimmed over the self-satisfied suits to a slim, streaky-haired blonde sitting behind a wide-shouldered man in a grey suit.

Déjà vu... He'd felt this a couple of times over the years— the tilt of a head, a sway of hips and his heart would stumble. When he took a second look he was always disappointed that it wasn't her.

Out of the corner of his eye Luke caught the movement of a slim hand sliding into bright hair, and the moisture in his mouth suddenly disappeared. He remembered those slim fingers, and his heart bashed against his ribcage as his eyes flew back to her hair, that wide mouth, the long, slim body under a deceptively simple but figure-revealing black dress. God, she looked good. Slimmer, sophisticated, with a tousled shoulder-length hairstyle that was hugely sexy. It accentuated her high cheekbones, her round dark eyes, that amazing mouth.

Luke hoped his poker face was in place… She couldn't— mustn't—suspect that she'd sent his pulse rocketing, his mind into overdrive and his libido into orbit. Luke gripped the podium as he waited for his knees to lock. He couldn't stop his eyes from tracking back to hers, and when they connected, volcanoes erupted. Jess's eyes, if you looked carefully enough, were the windows to her soul. Beneath the heat of their glances he knew that she was rattled.

Good. It went some way to making up for the uncomfortable and unwelcome fact that he still wanted her…which was such a foolish description for what he wanted to do to her, *with* her.

Luke blew out a heavy sigh. He knew why she was here. He wasn't a fool. Word was out that he was looking for a marketing strategy and she'd heard…and, being Jess, she was probably annoyed that he hadn't asked her.

Jess, again being Jess, didn't make appointments or pick up the phone to discuss it like a normal person. No, she rocked up here looking hot and sexy and very, very determined.

He wasn't sure whether to admire her cheek or be annoyed at her pushiness.

Luke cleared his throat and thought that he'd better get on with the business at hand.

'Ladies and gentlemen, this is probably going to be the shortest briefing in the history of the world. I want something new—something fresh that sells an enormous amount of wine. I want an overall marketing strategy, and then I want it broken down into website, social media, print and TV campaigns. All integrated. That's it. After your tour of the St Sylve cellars, Kendall de Villiers will take you through the market research report, and apparently there's a finger lunch and wine-tasting after that.'

Short and sweet. What else was there to say? He could have waffled on, but he was way more interested in having a very serious discussion with a certain brown-eyed blonde.

Jess slipped out of the tasting room after arranging for Ally to continue with the tour and get a lift back to the airport with Joel. She needed to slip away before she ran into Luke and was told that he wanted nothing to do with her. As she walked out she slipped on her knee-length black coat and pulled a thin silk scarf from its pocket. There was an icy wind blowing off the towering greeny-purple mountains that surrounded the estate. Jess walked down a path that snaked through the now denuded rose gardens, past the manor house and towards the long driveway where she'd parked her rental car.

Jess found a path between the manor house and the guest house. It led onto the driveway and Jess immediately saw

Luke, sitting on the top length of the pole fence that separated a winter-brown paddock from the driveway. Behind the paddock the vineyard started, and she could see his workers pruning the vines.

Jess stopped in the shadows of the house and just watched him.

He still fascinated her, Jess admitted. Oh, he was smoking hot, and he set her nerve-endings alight, but there was something beneath that attraction—something about him that engaged her internally as well. She knew he was smart, and she suspected that he could be ruthless, but it went deeper than simple pheromones and lust. Deep enough to have her mentally cocking her head.

One hundred percent alpha male and more than a match for her. The unwelcome thought popped into her head and settled. Jess stumbled, stopped and took a deep breath, and reminded herself that she was an alpha female and very able to deal with Luke Savage. She was an independent, successful, strong woman...

She was such a liar. Right now she felt as if she had all the inner strength of a marshmallow. She shouldn't be here at St Sylve, shouldn't be taking this project on. She really didn't need his business...

She especially didn't need the way he made her feel. Tingly, excited, a little unsure, a lot less confident.

Jess placed her hands on her waist and scowled at the ground. *Get a grip, Sherwood. You survived a childhood as the youngest girl with four older brothers, you run a successful business, you are independent, ambitious and in charge of this situation.*

You will not let him get under your skin...

Jess took a deep breath and stepped out of the shadows onto the driveway. Luke's head shot up. He jumped off the fence and pushed the sleeves of his T-shirt up his forearms as he scowled at her.

'Now, why aren't I surprised to see you here?' Luke asked in a very even tone.

Jess wasn't fooled. His green eyes were spitting spiders.

'Good to know you haven't lost any of your cheek.'

Sarcasm. He was still good at it.

Jess's rental car was parked closest to the fence and she dropped her laptop bag on the front seat, slammed the door shut and placed her bottom on the bonnet. She pushed her sunglasses into her hair and looked around.

As much as she wanted to, she would not get drawn into an argument right off the bat. Mostly because she wasn't sure she'd win it.

'I'd forgotten how beautiful this place is,' she commented idly, ignoring his opening volley. 'The air is so sweet, so pure. Cold, but sweet.'

Luke folded his arms as he loomed over her. 'What are you doing here, Jessica?'

Jess ignored his intimidation tactics and sent him a smile. 'I'm going to give you a marketing campaign that is going to blow your socks off, Luke.'

'Why? So you can say "I told you so"? To rub my face in the fact that I've failed? To push home the point that you, despite being so ridiculously young, were right?'

'No!' Jess put her hands on her hips and scowled at him. 'Why didn't you call me? Dammit, Luke. I know St Sylve. I know—'

Luke rubbed the back of his neck. He felt embarrassed and stupid and wished that she'd just leave him alone to try to fix the mess he'd made. Unfortunately his business brain also kept whispering that he'd be an idiot if he just sent her on her way without listening to her proposal.

There was a reason why she was reputed to be one of the best in the business…but why did she have to look even sexier than before?

The knowledge that he was still so attracted to her caused his temper to spike. 'You know *nothing*! You spent three months here eight years ago and you didn't know much then.'

'I want to help you…'

Luke shook his head. 'No, you don't. You want to make some money off me, do a deal, get the most sought-after contract around. You want to be proved right. You want to say "I told you so". You want to show me how clever you are.'

Jess shook her head. 'No, I— Come on, Luke, give me a break! I'm not the same cocky, over-zealous child I was eight years ago. I'm good at my job, and campaigns like yours are what I do best.'

Luke watched the heat of temper appear on her cheekbones, noticed the patches of red forming on her chest and neck. 'I don't need to watch you gloat. I have representatives of at least five other companies touring St Sylve right now, so they can—' Luke bent his fingers to emphasise the phrase '—"help" me.'

'I know that, but none of them are me. I've lived here, I've worked here, and I've always felt a connection to St Sylve. I can use that to create something special for you.'

She sounded sincere, Luke thought, but what did he know? He had vast experience of women—of people—turning sincerity on and off like a tap. Besides, he was tired and stressed and felt as if he'd been hit over the head by a two-by-four. 'Just go away, Jess.'

She lifted her chin and held his stare. 'No. Sorry, but, no. I *will* get the market research report and I *will* draw up a campaign for you. I don't care if you think I'm pushy or bossy or a pain in the butt—that is what is going to happen.'

Luke felt his temper bubble. 'Nothing has changed with you, has it? You're still over-confident and cocky—'

Jess hopped off the car, teetered on her heels and slapped her hand against his chest. Luke felt as if she'd branded him. He could see the pulse jumping at the base of her neck and noticed that her eyes had turned darker with…could that be embarrassment? Her obvious discomfort had his temper retreating.

'Can you be quiet for just a minute while I get this out?' Jess asked, her voice vibrating.

She seemed unaware that her hand was still on his chest, and although he lifted his hand to remove it, he didn't manage to complete the action. He rather liked her touching him…

Jess took a deep breath and raked tumbling hair back from her face with her other hand. 'I suck at apologising, so this might not come out right. But I'm really, really sorry for being so rude and revolting. I had no right to say the things I said to you, and you were right to fire me…in fact you did me a huge favour. I was intolerably cheeky and I'd really appreciate it if you accepted my apology.'

Huh? What? Luke frowned at her. That wasn't what he'd expected her to say…

'Are you apologising?' He just had to make sure. He'd had a tough couple of weeks. Maybe the stress was getting to him and he'd started imagining things.

Or maybe he just wanted to hear the words again.

Jess closed her eyes. 'Please don't make me say it again,' she begged. 'Once is embarrassing enough.'

Luke blew out his breath. 'What am I supposed to say to that?' he grumbled.

Jess made a sound that was a cross between a snort and a laugh.

'That you forgive me?' she suggested. 'That you'll let me design you a campaign that will sell an enormous amount of wine? That was an interesting briefing session, by the way. Short and—'

'Sweet?'

Jess's smile flashed. 'Just short. So? Can I?'

Luke, momentarily distracted by the tiny dimple that flashed in her cheek when she smiled, gathered his thoughts and told himself to be an adult. He couldn't just give her the campaign because she had a smile that made his belly clench, a body that begged to be touched and eyes he could drown in. Then again, it was *his* vineyard...

Get a grip, Savage.

'You can put in a tender for the job, along with everyone else.' Luke lifted up his hand when he saw Jess's face brighten. His next words were as much a warning to himself as they were to her. 'I'm not promising you a thing, Sherwood.'

Jess slowly nodded. 'Understood. Thank you. You won't regret this.'

Luke knew that on some level, at some time, he would.

Jess sent him a smile and a look that made his insides squirm with lust and, admittedly, fear.

'So, since I'm no longer trying to avoid you, and since I'm assuming that I'm not about to be tossed off the premises, I think I'll join the tour. Reacquaint myself with St Sylve.'

Luke, not keen to be inundated with questions from the rest of the suits but also not willing—*why?*—to leave Jess just yet, said, 'I'll walk you back to the cellar.'

'You don't have to,' Jess replied quickly. 'Besides, I was going to take the long route back—through the gardens and past the stables.'

Luke frowned. 'What on earth for?'

Jess lifted her shoulder. 'I have an idea for the campaign but I need to get a sense of St Sylve as it is now, not how I remember it.'

Luke lifted his eyebrows and looked at her sexy dress

and ridiculous heels. 'You want to walk in those shoes? That dress?'

Jess held out a foot and rotated it. 'What's wrong with my shoes? They're gorgeous.'

'But totally impractical for walking in—especially on farm roads. Take the path back, Jess.'

He could see her spine stiffening and her chin lifting. 'Thanks, but I'll take the circuitous route.'

Luke suppressed his smile at her stubbornness. Within twenty-five metres those spiky heels would be stuck in mud and her stockings would be flecked with dirt.

He gave Jess another up-and-down look and watched for her response. Her expression remained stoic while her eyes heated. He wondered what it would take to get her to lose the mask of sophistication she'd acquired.

He spoke casually. 'Do you ever think about what we did the last time we met?'

He didn't need to spell it out...she was a smart girl. Luke watched carefully and saw her composure slip for a fraction of a second, before her lips firmed and her eyes narrowed.

'No. Do you?'

'No,' Luke replied.

My, my, my, Luke thought as she walked away. *Look what good liars we've become.*

Jess, sitting on a hard seat at the airport, waiting for her flight to be called, looked at her shoes and grimaced. Once black, they were now streaked with reddish-brown mud and, she was certain, were beyond repair. Her stockings were splattered with runny sludge and dirty water. Her feet were aching from negotiating the uneven roads and paths at St Sylve in two-inch spikes and her toes had long since said goodbye to any feeling.

Damn Luke Savage for being right.

Jess felt her mobile vibrate in her hand and squinted down at the screen, where a message was displayed from the Sherwood family group.

John: Just to let you bunch of losers know that I ran 5K today in 24:30. Eat my dust, girls.

Jess had barely finished reading the message when a reply was posted.

Patrick: For an old guy, that's pretty good. But I run sub 24 routinely.

And they were off...

Chris: Liar! Your last race time was 30 mins plus.

Patrick: I had a stomach bug.

Nick: Prove it, squirt. You run like a girl. Even the Shrimp can take you down!

Patrick: I was sick! And Jess couldn't catch me with wings strapped to her back...

Jess, being the Shrimp and a girl, took offence at that. She was often faster than Patrick over five kilometres.

Jess: Hey, brainless...name the time and place and be prepared to watch my butt the whole way!

John: What are the stakes?

Jess wrinkled her nose. The last bet she'd lost to her brothers had ended up in her doing Chris's tax return. Maybe she hadn't thought this through.

Nick: A weekend cleaning out the monkey enclosure at the rehab centre for the loser.

Chris: Good one!

Eeew, thought Jess.

John: Hand-washing our rugby kit after practice.

Double *eeew.*

Liza AKA Mom: Now, now, children...play nice. Mommy's listening. And the loser will replace all the washers on my leaky taps. And they will not pay anyone to do this!

Jess twisted her lips. Unfortunately for her she knew how to wield a monkey wrench and thus would not be excused on account of gender. This was just another instance when she deeply regretted being a tomboy for most of her life.

And, really, when was she going to grow out of this absurd compulsion to prove that she was as big and as strong and as capable as her four older brothers? As a child she'd thought it deeply unfair that she'd been born a girl, and had decided early on that anything they could do she wanted to do better. So she'd studied hard and played harder in an effort to keep up with her siblings...and still always felt that she was on the outside of their 'brother circle' looking in. They were good-looking, charming, sporty and successful—a very annoying bunch of over-achievers... She thought that Luke would fit in very well with them.

The bet was madness, Jess thought, frowning at her feet and wondering how to get out of it. And as for her gorgeous shoes...they were history.

CHAPTER THREE

JESS'S THIN HEELS made tiny square marks in the thick carpet of the passage outside the smallest conference room at the hotel where Luke had chosen to view the various campaign presentations. She was scheduled to present last, and was getting more and more nervous. Realising that her hands were slick with perspiration, she hustled off to the closest bathroom to wash her hands and check her face. *Again.*

She was being ludicrous, she decided, drying her hands for the third time in twenty minutes. Since her *contretemps* with Luke eight years ago she'd always been nervous before presentations, but no one besides Ally ever knew it. She appeared to be ice-cool and confident, unflappable, but underneath her façade her heart misfired and her brain spluttered.

Jess slicked on another layer of lipstick and smoothed down her scarlet mid-thigh-length jacket. The bottom of her short black pencil skirt just peeked out under the hem, and she wore a black silk polo-neck jersey underneath. With sheer black stockings and knee-high boots, the outfit was dramatic and eye-catching, and not what she'd usually wear to pitch for a job.

But if this was the last time she'd see Luke Savage then she'd damn well make sure that she made a lasting impression.

Ally stuck her head around the door to the Ladies'. 'Jess, it's time.'

Jess walked out of the Ladies' and was grateful for Ally's steadying hand on her back, unaware that she was biting the inside of her lip. 'Let's knock their socks off.'

'Okay…but maybe you should take a deep breath first…'

'Why?' Jess asked, picking up her laptop and boards.

'Your knees are knocking together.' Ally reached into her bag and pulled out a small bottle of Rescue Remedy. 'Open up.'

'Ally!' Jess muttered, but she obediently stuck out her tongue as Ally shook the foul-tasting drops into her mouth.

The door behind them opened and Jess's eyes slid over. She winced as Luke stepped out of the conference room.

'Hi—' He stopped suddenly and Jess yanked her tongue in. Could she feel any more stupid?

'What on earth are you doing?' Luke demanded, his hands in the pockets of his smart black pants. Jess noticed his button-down cream shirt with its discreet, expensive logo and sighed at how good he looked.

Mr Savage cleaned up very, very well indeed.

'Nothing,' Jess muttered.

'Rescue Remedy,' Ally said at the same time. 'Jess tends to get a bit nervous before presentations.'

'Alison!'

Luke smiled at Jess and her stomach flipped over. 'I would never have guessed. Jess doesn't seem to be the gets-nervous type.' Luke held out his hand to Alison. 'Luke Savage.'

'Ally Davies.' Ally shook his hand.

'How nervous?' Luke asked, and Jess willed Ally not to be her normal open, brutally honest self.

'Very. Her knees are knocking together and her hands are shaking.'

'Will you stop?' Jess demanded. 'Jeez, Alison! He's a client.'

'Relax, Jess, there's no need to torture such pretty knees.'

Luke sent her another of his slow, sexy smiles that were guaranteed to melt the panties off any female between eighteen and eighty. It was the smile she intended to use to launch his campaign. She was under no illusions. It was going to be tough to sell it to him...

'And I like the skirt you're almost wearing, Sherwood,' Luke added.

'Oh, shut up!' Jess told him before sailing into the room, her nose up in the air.

Great start, Jess, telling your prospective client to put a cork in it. Not.

Jess ended her presentation and caught herself biting the inside of her lip in the resultant heavily pregnant silence. She felt her heart thumping in her chest and wondered if the St Sylve contingency could hear it.

Thump, thump, kadoosh. Thump, thump... Oh, the *kadoosh* happened every time she looked at Luke; it was, Jess realised, her heart bouncing off the floor.

Well, okay, then. Good to know. Better if she knew how to make it *stop*.

Luke looked utterly inscrutable and non-committal—especially for somebody who, as she'd suggested, should be the new face of St Sylve wines. Did they love it? Hate it? Think that she'd not only crossed the line but redrawn it as well? Jess just wished they'd say something—*anything*!

About a million years later—okay, ten seconds, but it felt that long—Luke sat forward and rested his arms on the table. His eyes sliced through her.

'Let me get this straight... You want me to be the face of St Sylve?'

Jess nodded. 'Not just the face of St Sylve. I want the consumer to associate you and St Sylve with fun. Hip and cool, yet sophisticated. The plan isn't to sell your wine. It's to sell your life.'

Now Luke looked thoroughly puzzled. 'I don't have a life, Jessica! I work and that's about it!'

'The consumer doesn't know that, Luke. He sees you as this young, single, good-looking—' *smoking hot,* but she couldn't say that '—rich guy who has the world at his feet. He does hip and cool things…like parasailing, dancing, mountain-climbing. He plays touch rugby with his mates, has friends around for dinner, attends balls. And it's all done with, or followed by, a glass of wine. St Sylve wine.'

'I love it,' Kendall said. 'I think it's brilliant.'

Jess flashed him a grateful smile.

'I like the idea, but I don't like the idea of me doing it. Why can't you get a model to…model?' Luke demanded.

'It would have a bigger impact if the owner of the winery appeared in the adverts and, frankly—' Jess took a deep breath '—why would you want to spend a shedload of cash on a model when you are attractive enough to do it yourself?'

And I managed to say that without blushing or drooling, Jess thought.

'I'm really liking this,' Kendall stated.

'Actually, so am I,' Owen agreed, but Jess noticed that he wasn't looking at her but at Ally. Okay, so that was interesting. Jess swivelled her head. Ally was *so* looking back, the flirt!

Luke stood up abruptly. 'Thanks, everybody. It's been a long day. Let's sleep on it and meet on Monday to make a decision. Jess, if you'd wait, I'd like a moment of your time?'

Now *he wants a moment,* Jess thought. He's had three weeks. She looked at Luke, who was writing on her presentation booklet. Then again, it was probably about work.

She was acting like a lonely, lovelorn teenager. She was, it was embarrassing to admit, an utter drip.

* * *

Luke waited until the last person had left the room and the door had snicked closed behind them before walking around the table to the top of the room, where Jess was still standing by the projector screen, a laser pointer in her hand. He sat on the edge of the boardroom table and stretched out his legs. Jess seemed to get better-looking each time he saw her, he thought idly. She'd done something to her hair—there were now pale blonde streaks in the honey colour. It was also brutally straight today. He preferred it loose and curly...

Luke scratched his forehead, thinking that he was too far gone if he was wasting time noticing the details of a woman's hair. Which was chilling on a dozen different levels.

He was impressed with her presentation, her professionalism; no one would have guessed that this slick, cool businesswoman suffered from performance anxiety. He wouldn't have guessed it if he hadn't seen her sticking her tongue out for those drops. The entire episode made her seem not quite so aloof, a little warmer, a lot more human. Infinitely attractive.

'Um...what do you really think about my idea?' Jess asked, and he could hear a quiver underneath her professional tone of voice.

'I like it—apart from me being in the ads.'

'I should also tell you that I think you should start getting out, promoting the St Sylve name and its wine. I would strongly suggest that you go out more...social events, parties, balls...and that you host wine-tasting evenings and start networking.'

'Why don't you just take my internal organs? It would be easier.' Luke rubbed the back of his neck. 'Do you have an extra twenty-four hours in the day for me?'

'It's important, Luke.'

'I don't have the time, Jess. I'm working at St Sylve. I get home from the land and then I spend hours on business plans, financing… I'm running my other businesses at night. I don't have the time for advertising shoots, let alone for a social life.'

'Then I think you should be prepared to keep ploughing your own money into St Sylve or to lose it,' Jess told him bluntly. 'You need the wines to sell to get St Sylve sustainable, and to do that you need sales—for sales you need advertising.'

'Then why must I do the social stuff?'

'Because you need to be seen to be living the campaign or else the consumers won't believe in it.' Jess perched on the edge of the conference table and crossed her legs. 'Step out of your comfort zone, Luke.'

Comfort zone? He hadn't felt remotely comfortable since he'd set eyes on her again weeks ago.

Luke eyed her long legs in those sexy boots and felt his groin twitch. *Dammit!* He didn't like not being able to control his physical reaction to this woman, the fact that he thought about her far too often. And he especially didn't like the fact that she could talk so coolly about business when he was imagining her naked except for those boots, at the mercy of his touch…

'If I agree to hire you, and by doing so agree to any and all of your proposals,' he said in a voice that most of his staff and friends would recognise as non-negotiable, 'then I have a couple of conditions of my own.'

'Okay—what?'

'*You* work on the campaign. No passing it off to your flunkies.'

'Understood. I had no intention of doing that anyway.'

'And I want St Sylve to have your undivided attention. You move to St Sylve for however long it takes to get this wrapped up. Get out of *your* comfort zone.'

He saw the look of shock that flicked across her face. 'That's not practical, Luke. I have a business to run.'

'Skype, e-mail and phone. We live in the twenty-first century, Jess. Besides, Ally looks competent enough to take the reins.'

'She is, but—'

'And you also organise the networking. I don't have the time or the inclination and I have even less enthusiasm. And you accompany me to all these functions. If I have to do it, then so do you,' Luke told her.

'So, are you saying I've got the job?'

'Yep.'

Of course she had the job—was she mad? Hers was above and beyond the most exciting presentation of them all, and while the others wouldn't need his time, presence or input, they wouldn't have the effect Jess's would.

'Uh...good,' Jess said in a strangled voice. 'But I don't know if I'm going to manage living in Franschoek. I have a life, apart from my business, in Sandton.'

Luke shook his head. No, she didn't. She was as much a workaholic as him. 'Stop hedging. And you're not staying in Franschoek—you're staying at St Sylve.'

Jess thrust out her stubborn chin. 'I won't feel comfortable staying with you, in your house.'

'Why not?'

Jess rolled her eyes. 'Are you really going to be all coy and not acknowledge the...'

Luke lifted his eyebrows when she stuttered to a stop. 'Lust? Heat? Passion?' he suggested.

'Heat...stick to heat,' Jess suggested, her eyes everywhere but meeting his.

Luke grinned internally; it amazed him that she could be so businesslike about—well, *business*, but get so flustered when talking about their mutual attraction.

'Now who's being coy?' Luke muttered. 'Okay, you can stay in any one of the six bedrooms at the manor house.'

Luke stepped closer—so close he could almost feel her

breasts against his chest, smell the citrus in her hair. Those amazingly long lashes fluttered and lifted and he felt the zing of attraction arc between them. In that age-old subconscious display of attraction her mouth opened, and he nearly lost control when he saw the tip of her pink tongue flicker at the corner of her mouth. Stuff the marketing strategy and St Sylve. Stuff the world...Jess was here and he wanted her.

Her body, not her mind...

Luke jerked his head up and quietly cursed. And what was he doing? Acting on what was happening in his pants. *Catch a clue, Savage.* He wasn't fifteen any more, or even twenty, but he was still listening to his libido. He'd realised a while back that it was a very bad judge of character, time and situation, and it had the ability to lead him into deep trouble.

Luke stepped away from Jess, but couldn't resist tucking a long, straight strand of hair behind her ear. 'Don't disappoint me, Jess.'

'I don't intend to,' she replied in her husky, take-me-to-bed voice.

Jess finally looked him in the eye and he couldn't help himself; his thumb drifted across her bottom lip. 'You have the most kissable mouth I've ever seen.'

He saw sense and sensibility flow back into Jess's eyes— her mental retreat. A cool, polite mask dropped into place.

'Not a good idea, Luke. Any physical intimacy could blow up in our faces.'

'We should be smart enough to separate the two.'

Her shoulders came up and her spine stiffened at his challenge. 'Theoretically I'm smart enough—anybody is smart enough—to solve string theory, but that doesn't mean I can. Or will.'

'We have unfinished business, Jessica. You know it and I know it; we both want to finish what we started eight years ago.' Luke moved the backs of his fingers down her cheek.

Jess's eyes remained passionate even as she nudged his hand away. 'Luke, let me make it very clear that I don't do casual sex—especially not with colleagues, competitors or clients.'

He loved the snap he heard in her voice, the passion that slumbered in her eyes. The contradiction of the two had his heart in his throat and his groin twitching. This was going to be interesting, he thought, amused and still very turned on. She might be flustered but she wasn't intimidated, and she didn't back down.

He wondered who'd taught her that.

The day before Jess was due to arrive at St Sylve, Luke sat on the end of the antique double bed in the largest guest suite in the manor house and looked around the room. Angel, his part-time housekeeper, had worked her magic in the room he'd allocated Jess. The yellow wood headboard had been oiled, there was white linen on the bed and fresh flowers on the nightstand. Luke glanced through the large bay window opposite the bed which enabled the guest to wake to a stunning view of the mountains. Luke had never understood why this room, with its large *en-suite* bathroom, had never been used as the master bedroom instead of the smaller, pokier bedroom at the front of the house, overlooking the driveway.

Easier to see who was coming up the road, Luke decided. Friend, foe, tax collector... In his father's case, lover. There had been many, Luke knew. He remembered lots of women wafting around the house when he was a child... Some had paid far too much attention to him; others had paid him absolutely no attention at all.

They'd all left eventually. By the age of seven he'd learned to protect himself against getting emotionally attached to any of his father's girlfriends. That way he hadn't been affected when they'd dropped out of his life. Apart from the blip that had been his marriage, it was his standard operating procedure when it came to women.

Being a reasonably astute guy, he hadn't needed therapy to work out that he'd learnt to protect himself against emotional entanglements, and he'd honed his ability to keep his distance from people at a young age. Between his mother's death, his father's dictator tendencies and his girlfriends wafting in and then storming out, it had become easier not to care whether people left or not.

His ex-wife and his marriage had been the exception to that rule. While he now called her a crazoid, with the ability to incinerate money, he had to accept that his own issues had also contributed to the train wreck. He hadn't loved her, but he'd been monstrously in love with the *idea* of her: a wife, a family, normality. When he'd got it he hadn't known what to do with it…

Saying goodbye to his lifelong dream of being part of something bigger than himself had stung like a shark bite, and because Fate had thought that wasn't punishment enough, his father had died and he'd been yanked back to St Sylve.

He was still trying to come to terms with his legacy, and frequently wasn't sure how he felt about the estate. Some days he loved it. Then resentment got the better of him, and on other days, when the memories of his father bubbled close to the surface, he actively hated the place.

If only his mother had— Luke stomped over to the window and looked at the mountains in the near distance. There was no point in thinking about his mother, Jed and his childhood. Nothing he could do to change it.

Luke sighed and thought of Jess. He knew that she was right—that the intelligent decision would be to ignore this attraction bubbling away. He knew that when the lines between working and sleeping together were blurred, confusion and craziness generally followed.

But she was a modern, independent woman—one who didn't appear to need a man for emotional or financial support to make her life complete. She appeared to be controlled, thinking, cool—someone who could separate love from sex. A perfect candidate for a short-term affair.

She would understand that there would have to be rules. No sleep-overs, a strict division between work and play, no expectations of commitment or a relationship.

It was all in the communication, Luke decided. As long as they both understood the rules, no one would get hurt or could complain.

It was the adult, rational, sensible solution. And if she stuck to her guns and maintained that she couldn't, *wouldn't*, sleep with a client, then he'd do what any rational, determined man would do.

He'd seduce her into it. With the heat they generated, he didn't think it would be too difficult.

Thirteen hours in a car gave a girl lots of time to get her mind sorted, Jess thought as she turned down the long driveway leading to St Sylve. It was nearly ten at night and she was utterly exhausted. Her eyes were gritty, her body stiff, and she could murder a cup of tea.

She'd initially thought she'd take two days to do the trip, but when she'd reached halfway she'd thought she would push through. She now wished she'd stopped. She had a massive headache and, although she'd done nothing all day but steer, she felt dirty and sweaty. Her hair was unbrushed and her teeth felt as if they were dripping enamel from the energy drinks she'd chain-drunk earlier.

Jess saw lights blazing from the guest house, and when she saw Luke's Land Cruiser parked in the driveway she knew that he was home and not out on a date or—*eeew*—a sleep-over. Thank goodness.

Right. Before she saw him again, a quick recap on all she'd decided during the day. Living and working so closely with Luke was going to be a challenge. She got that. He was gorgeous, and she was crazy-mad attracted to him, but she couldn't act on it.

'No acting on the attraction.' She muttered her new mantra. 'No acting on the attraction.' She just needed to say it forty times a day—an hour?—and her brain would be reprogrammed. Maybe.

When she wasn't so tired she'd sit him down and lay out some simple ground rules. She was here to do a job, so kissing and touching and most especially sleeping together were out. She'd didn't sleep with her clients. It was unprofessional. And when trouble brewed it always mucked up the business relationship. Always.

Besides that, attraction spilt over into involvement, which tended to make her end up feeling as if she'd tossed her heart to a pack of rabid, starving wolves.

Luke would just have to understand that for the next few weeks he might own her time, but her body wasn't included in the deal. Her body, slutty thing that it was, wasn't very impressed with that decision. *Tough.* Someone had to be the adult…

In the light of her headlights she saw the front door of the guest house open and Luke's tall silhouette in the doorway. She parked her car next to his Cruiser and switched off her iPod, playing through the car speakers. Hard rock stopped mid-wail and there was blessed silence in the car. Why hadn't she done that earlier? Oh, right—the edgy album had kept her from falling asleep and drifting off the road.

Jess released the seat belt as Luke opened her door. She smiled wearily up at him, her eyes wide and blinking against the interior light. 'Hi.'

Luke rested his arm on the top of the car and stood in the doorway. Instead of giving her a smile and a warm greeting, she saw his face was hard in the dim light. 'When did you leave home?' he barked.

That wasn't a friendly woof. Jess frowned. No *hello*? No *good to see you*?

'Uh…this morning,' Jess replied. 'Is that a problem?'

'Damn right it is,' Luke whipped back. 'What do you think you are doing, driving thirteen hours straight? Without letting anyone know? If you'd had an accident how would I have known? You could be lying in a ditch somewhere and I'd still think you'd be arriving tomorrow!'

Jess blinked at his tirade. 'Uh–'

'Did you let *anyone* know?' Luke demanded, increasing his volume with every word.

'No, I—'

'It's stupid and irresponsible. Do you know what can happen to a woman driving on her own?'

'They arrive safely?' Jess asked, her temper starting to bubble.

'You could've hit a cow, broken down, had a puncture…'

Jess spoke in her coldest voice as she stepped out of the car. 'I'm a grown woman who doesn't need to check in like a child. I didn't break down, have a puncture or—good grief!—hit a cow! I am here safely. I want a cup of tea, a shower and a warm bed. Can I get any or all of those, or do you need to yell at me some more?'

'You would try the patience of a flipping saint.'

'And that saint wouldn't be you,' Jess snapped back. She opened the back door and yanked a large tote bag from the seat. Luke took the bag and Jess reached for it. 'I can carry my own bag!'

'Fine.' Luke dropped the bag to the ground and held up

his hands. This woman was going to drive him nuts, up the wall…

Jess picked up her bag, slung it over her shoulder and squinted at the dark manor house. 'No lights?'

'Obviously not. Since I was expecting you *tomorrow*!'

He'd planned on switching on the electrics and the geyser feeding her bathroom in the manor house in the morning, so he supposed he'd have to install her in his tiny guest bedroom/storeroom for the night.

Joy of joys. How was he supposed to sleep, imagining her in a bed not more than a thirty-second walk from his own?

'Can we possibly go inside?' Jess asked, her voice as cold as the wind that blew off the mountains.

Luke gestured to his house and followed her long legs in loose jeans. In low boots, with her stripy hair and belligerent expression, she looked like an angry owl. A *sexy* angry owl…

Luke shook his head as her shoulder dropped with the weight of the bag but resisted the urge to take it off her shoulder. Why was he was feeling so annoyed? Protectiveness? Could that be what it was?

Well, *damn*.

He'd always felt uneasy about her travelling across the country on her own, but since she'd planned to do the trip over two days, and would be driving during daylight hours, he'd told himself that she would be fine. When he'd seen her white face and blue-shadowed eyes in the light of her SUV he'd felt a rush of relief followed by a tidal wave of anger because she'd pushed herself so hard to get to St Sylve—driving those passes through the mountains while tired was simple stupidity. He was mad because protectiveness was a precursor to caring, and caring was a precursor to getting involved— which led to pain when someone left, and that wasn't something he was prepared to have happen again.

So… *Take a deep breath, Savage.* He had to find his self-control, get some distance between him and this fascinating woman.

And while he'd been a bit blasé about wanting her in his bed, now, with her arrival, he was rethinking that. Not that he didn't want her in his bed—he still wanted that as much as he wanted his heart to keep pumping—but he was thinking that if he saw her as someone he felt protective over instead of an independent, competent woman there could be massive complications down the road.

Was sleeping with her worth the complications? He really wished he knew.

Luke scowled at Jess's slow-moving figure. Apart from putting his libido on speed, she made his breath hitch and his heart stutter. He thought about her when she wasn't there and felt protective over her, though she was perfectly capable of looking after herself, and worst of all his world made much more sense now that she was here at St Sylve.

Luke blew out a frustrated breath; he was losing it, he decided. Years of working far too hard and playing far too little were catching up to him. Luke caught her low groan as she moved the tote bag from one arm to another. Frustrated at her independence, he stepped up and yanked the bag from her grasp.

Jess started to protest, but something on his face had the words dying on her lips.

Excellent. He was making progress.

For about ten seconds.

'I'm a modern, self-sufficient woman who doesn't need a man to carry stuff for her or lecture her on road safety!' Jess told him as he opened his front door and stood back to let her precede him.

Progress? One step forward, six back...

'Yeah, yeah—blah, blah. Just get inside the house, Sherwood, and stop being a pain in my ass,' Luke told her—and wondered if he had enough wine on the estate to take the edge off the frustration he felt when he was around this woman.

Probably not.

CHAPTER FOUR

EARLY THE NEXT MORNING, Luke stood with Owen on the veranda of his house, two massive Rhodesian Ridgebacks lying at their feet. Both men held hot cups of coffee—a welcome relief after the freezing temperatures in the lands.

Owen lifted his mug at the magnificent Dutch-gabled manor house directly across from them. 'You've got to admit it's one hell of a building.'

Luke nodded. 'My ancestors were quite determined to make a statement that this was Savage land and that they mattered. Except for my father a seven-bedroom manor house wasn't spacious enough. So he ordered the building of my house as a smaller guest house.' Jed had also converted the carriage house into an office block, installed a gym, Jacuzzi and steam room, refurbished the tennis court, relandscaped the gardens...

'All on borrowed money,' Owen commented.

'Yep—money he didn't have and St Sylve couldn't generate.'

After his father's death Luke had immediately sold anything that wasn't nailed down—excluding the family silver and furniture—to pay off his father's debts. The money received had barely made a dent in the debt he'd inherited along with St Sylve.

Frankly, it would have been cheaper to buy his own wine

farm…oh, wait, he *had*. He'd bought and paid for his own inheritance. If he added up all the money he'd poured into the estate over the years, servicing the debt and the interest, he'd probably paid three times what it was worth.

'My father was intensely concerned about the image he portrayed. It didn't matter that he was on the verge of losing everything. As long as the illusion of perfection was maintained he was content.' Luke shrugged. 'Sometimes I feel like going beyond the grave and slapping him stupid.'

'Can I come too?' Owen asked.

'Who is going where?'

Both men turned quickly, and Luke's cup wobbled as he saw Jess standing in the doorway of his house, dressed in jeans and low boots, her face mostly free of make-up and her hair pulled into a messy knot.

Luke felt his stomach clench and release.

After he'd introduced her to Owen and they'd exchanged some small talk, Owen glanced at his watch and excused himself. Luke thought that he needed to get back to the lands too, but he felt reluctant to leave Jess. It wasn't good manners just to leave her on her own, he told himself…*lied* to himself.

'We need to get your stuff into the manor house. I switched the electrics on; you now have lights but it'll be a couple of hours until you get hot water.'

'Thanks.' Jess wrinkled her nose. 'I'll do that later. I want to explore St Sylve, if that's okay.'

'Sure.' Luke shrugged. 'I'll give you a tour. What do you want to see?'

Jess shrugged. 'Everything.'

'Everything?'

'I know the cellars and the buildings. I want to see the lands and the vineyard and the orchards.'

'Okay.'

Luke stepped into the house and deposited the coffee cups on the hall table. Yanking down a heavy jacket from the rack behind the door, he handed it to Jess, thinking of how icy it could get on the bike. He pulled on his own battered wool-lined leather jacket over his long-sleeved T-shirt and stuffed a beanie into one of the pockets. In the shadows of the mountains the temperature could drop rapidly.

'If you want to tag along, I need to check on how far along my staff are with the pruning, then I need to go across the farm to check on repairs to a fence.'

Luke gestured to his powerful dirt bike and led her towards it.

'My Land Cruiser has gone in for a service, and the farm truck has gone to town, so this is the only mode of transport I have at the moment.' Luke slung his leg over the bike. 'Hop on. Relax and don't fight me. Do you want a helmet?'

Jess sent him a cocky grin before sliding on behind him. 'No, I want my own bike.'

'You ride?' Luke asked, not able to imagine this city slicker in charge of a dirt bike.

'I have four older brothers. I ride, fish, surf, play one hell of a game of touch rugby, can start my own fire for a barbecue and change a tyre,' Jess said as she settled herself on the bike, her thighs warm against his hips, her breasts against his back.

Oh, hell, she sounded like the perfect woman. That was *not* good. Luke turned the key and the bike roared to life.

'Oh—and the faster the better!' Jess yelled in his ear. Luke grinned as he picked up speed. 'Yee-hah!'

Luke felt her hands, light on his hips, and smelt the occasional whiff of something sexy from her perfume. He knew that she was smiling, and when her body relaxed he realised that her tension had disappeared.

Luke felt the wind on his face, her warmth at his back

and felt...*content*? He let the thought roll around his head... contentment.

No, probably not. And even if it was, experience had taught him that it wouldn't last.

It was mid-afternoon before Luke turned the bike to head back to St Sylve, and Jess was past frozen. A cold front had rapidly moved in, with an icy wind that had blown in heavy clouds and was sneaking in under her clothes. Jess buried her face in between Luke's shoulderblades and gripped his hips with now frozen hands. She wished she felt comfortable enough to slide her hands up under his jacket to get her hands out of the freezing wind.

Jess pulled her head up as Luke braked and stopped the bike. He left it idling as he half turned to face her. He took her hands in his and rubbed them.

'I can feel you shivering. Sorry, I didn't mean to keep you out this long,' Luke said, blowing his hot breath onto her hands.

Jess quivered and not only because of the cold. Seeing that dark head bent over her hands and feeling his warm breath on her skin made the worms squirm in her stomach.

'How long until we're back?' Jess asked, her teeth chattering.

Luke winced. 'About forty minutes. This cold front came up really quickly.' He looked up and frowned at the black clouds gathering above. 'We might get wet.'

Jess shrugged. 'Well, then, we'd better get moving.'

Luke pulled a black-and-white beanie out of his pocket and pulled it over her ears, tucking away her hair. They were close enough to kiss, Jess thought. She could count each individual spiky eyelash, could see the gold highlights in his very green eyes, could make out the faint traces of a scar in his left eyebrow.

She really wanted to be kissed…

Luke's fingers were cool on her face as he tucked her hair under the cap and she wondered if she imagined his fingers lingering for a moment longer than necessary on her cheekbone.

'At the risk of you taking this the wrong way, get as close as possible. Put your hands under my jacket—get them warm. The temperature is dropping fast,' Luke said as he turned back.

Luke waited while she wriggled herself as close to him as she could and until her hands were flat on his stomach—oh, the blessed warmth—before roaring off. Jess put her face back between his shoulderblades and felt so much more comfortable than she had just minutes before.

His stomach was hard and ridged with muscle and his back was broad, protecting her from the wind they were now riding into. She'd forgotten how much of a man he was, Jess thought as the first drops of icy rain fell. It wasn't only his impressive body—while he wasn't muscle bound, he was still ripped in all the right places, like the six-pack under her hands—but wherever he went on the estate he instantly commanded respect.

She'd watched and listened as he interacted with his staff. He gave orders easily, listened when he needed to and made swift decisions. His employees felt at ease around him— enough to crack jokes and initiate conversation.

She hadn't realised how extensive his property was or how much he was responsible for. He had a small dairy herd that provided milk to a processing dairy in town, orchards that exported plums and soft citrus, and olives that were sold to a factory in Franschoek that pressed and bottled olive oil.

'They all add to the St Sylve coffers,' Luke had said, a muscle jumping in his jaw. 'Thank God.'

'Are the St Sylve coffers empty?' she'd joked.

'You have no idea.'

Jess couldn't understand it...*why* did St Sylve have money troubles if he had all these other sources of income? Even if the wine wasn't selling that well, then the milk and olives, sheep and fruit should subsidise the winery.

It was a puzzle. Jess felt a big drop of rain hit her cheek and she shivered. Luke briefly placed his left hand over her hands, as if to reassure her, and Jess rubbed her cheek against his back and turned her thoughts back to St Sylve.

Luke and St Sylve were such a conundrum. According to the grapevine, Luke made money hand over fist from his venture capital business, so he was supposedly not hurting for cash. It was common knowledge that he had extensive business interests apart from St Sylve, and he was reputed to have the very fortunate ability to make money—a lot of which, she suspected, he poured into this estate. Although he was based in Franschoek she knew that he provided financial and management capital to high-potential, high-risk, high-growth startup companies for a stake in said company.

But the question remained: if he had all these other sources of income for the farm and he was still selling wine—not huge amounts, but enough—why would he imply that the farm was in the red? That it wasn't self-supporting?

It was very bewildering.

Jess silently cursed as the rain started to fall in earnest. Within a minute the drops had turned into icy bullets that soaked her jeans and ran down her neck into her jersey. Jess groaned. She'd look like a frozen drowned rat by the time she got back to St Sylve...

'Are you okay?' Luke yelled at her.

I'm cold and I'm wet, Jess thought, but Luke knew that already. What was the point in whining? 'I'm okay. Could murder a cup of coffee, though!'

'You and me both. Damn Cape weather!' Luke shouted, and Jess just caught his words before the wind whipped them away.

'There's ice in the rain,' Jess yelled in his ear. She knew this because she could feel ice in the drop that was rolling down her spine towards her panties. She resisted the urge to wiggle.

'I wasn't going to mention it,' Luke stated as he abruptly stopped the bike.

'Why are you stopping?' Jess demanded. 'I thought the point was to get home as quick as possible!'

'It is.' Luke looked at a small track leading off from the dirt road. 'How are you at cross-country?'

'I've done it.' Jess looked at him and pursed her lips. 'Will it get us home quicker?'

'It'll save us about twenty minutes. But it's tough. And muddy. And it'll mean going through a small stream.'

Jess shrugged. 'I'm soaked already. Let's do it.'

Luke squeezed her thigh. 'You're quite a package, Sherwood. And even more of a surprise.'

Jess wasn't sure if that was a compliment or not.

Luke had already polished off one cup of coffee and was on his second when Jess walked into the kitchen, dressed in another pair of jeans and a dark blue jersey.

'Coffee?' he asked, even as he poured her a cup.

'God, yes.' Jess took the cup, wrapped her hands around it and sipped. 'Oh, that's heavenly.' Jess took a seat at the wooden four-seater table in the centre of the room and sipped and sighed. When her eyes met his, she smiled. 'One hell of a tour, Savage.'

'I'm really sorry we got caught in the storm,' Luke said. It wasn't like him. He always paid attention. But his mind had been on Jess and his hyper-awareness of her. The way her body had felt against his, listening to her introduce herself to his staff and engage them in conversation, watching her as she suddenly stopped walking and just looked off into the distance, as if she were taking a mental snapshot.

She was a city girl, and her attitude today had impressed him and, if he were one hundred percent honest, thrown him off his stride. He'd expected her to whine and moan about being wet and cold, yet she'd sucked it up and said nothing, accepting that there was nothing he could do about the situation but get them home as quickly as possible. While he'd pushed the bike through mud and grass and that icy stream she'd said nothing to disturb his concentration, and he'd got them back in record time...wet and dirty but ultimately safely, and as quickly as he possibly could.

She hadn't griped or complained.

'My boots are covered in mud. At least I can clean these— unlike my suede heels that I had to toss.'

Luke's smile flashed. 'I told you so. You'll have to get a pair of gumboots.'

Jess shuddered. 'They are so incredibly ugly.'

Luke rolled his eyes. 'But made for mud and rain.'

Jess placed her cup on the table and looked past him to the window. 'It's really belting down.'

'Winter in the Cape,' Luke said. 'Want some more coffee?'

'Not just yet,' Jess replied. 'Thanks for the tour. I've already got some good ideas for the campaign...'

'Want to share them with me?' He took a seat at the table, propping his feet up on the seat of the nearest chair.

'Not yet. Still percolating.'

'So tell me why you wanted to work for me.' After what had happened between them he'd thought that she'd hold a grudge for ever. 'Why *did* you gatecrash my party, Jess?'

Jess rolled her cup between her palms. 'It's the most talked-about campaign around and I'm competitive enough to want to snag it. That was one reason. Another is that I have a reputation in the industry…I'm becoming very well known for tackling hard-to-rescue brands or campaigns. And I have a soft spot for St Sylve and this type of campaign is what I do best.'

'Even though I—?'

'Fought with me, kissed me and then fired me?' A small smile tipped the corners of Jess's mouth upward. 'I deserved everything you said to me. You were right to fire me, and the k— Well, it was all a long time ago.'

She'd been about to mention the kiss, Luke realised. He really wished he knew what she wanted to say about it. That it was fantastic? She wanted to do it again? They'd be amazing in bed? It *had* been fantastic, he *did* want to do it again and, yes, he wanted her in his bed.

Jess was staring at his mouth and he wondered if she was remembering that afternoon so long ago, how it had felt to be in his arms, her breasts mashed against his chest, his tongue in her warm, tasty mouth. Luke heaved in a deep breath and surreptitiously dropped his hand beneath the table to quickly rearrange his package. It seemed that Jess still had the same effect on him as she had all those years ago.

He was coming to realise that he really didn't want to be attracted to this woman. He felt that she could, if he wasn't very, very careful, be a threat to his emotional self-sufficiency, his resolve not to become emotionally entangled.

Sleeping with her wasn't worth the price that he would have to pay if he found himself emotionally trapped. And that was why she shouldn't be sitting in his kitchen on a rainy Sunday looking sweet and hot, relaxed and rosy. She looked far too enticing…

Luke shoved his chair back and abruptly stood up. 'Listen, I can't sit around and drink coffee all day. I need to get into my office.'

Jess lifted her eyebrows. 'No rest for the wicked? Even on a Sunday?'

'I'm still running another company…I have to take what time I can get.' Luke gestured to the fridge and raked his fingers through his hair. 'Help yourself to whatever you can find to eat if you're hungry. When the storm lets up I'll help you move into the manor house. There's a TV in the lounge, or…'

Jess shrugged. 'I'll grab my computer from the room and do some work myself.'

Luke shoved his hands into his pockets, desperately wishing he could just drag her upstairs to bed. 'Well, call me if you need anything.'

Jess nodded. 'I'll be fine, Luke. I always am.'

It was the first time in the history of the world that a film crew had been on time for anything, Jess thought as she roared up Luke's driveway to see the vehicles of the film company outside Luke's front door. Behind them she could see the portly figure of her favourite director, Sbu, the willow-thin stylist, Becca, and she recognised one of the two cameramen.

She hadn't planned to shoot the first ad only two nights after she'd arrived at St Sylve, but, as Owen had said, the pruning was nearly done and if she wanted to capture Luke working on vines that had some foliage on them she'd have to get moving. It was fortuitous that Sbu and his team were free today—well, they had planned on some editing, but she'd persuaded, bribed, threatened them into coming to St Sylve instead.

Jess sat in her car for a moment, knowing that the next couple of hours were going to be madness. She needed five minutes to gather her wits…

She was now officially installed in the manor house, in a beautiful bedroom with an attached study and large bathroom.

After the storm had abated Luke had helped her move her

mountains of luggage up to her room and then disappeared back into his office. Later she'd heard him leave on the dirt bike. She'd heard him come back around seven, and when he hadn't wandered over, she'd decided that she was too tired to deal with him anyway and tumbled into the enormous bed.

She hadn't seen him since, and thought the chances of her having to go yank him out of the lands were quite high.

Or not, Jess thought as she jumped out of her car. There he was, talking to Sbu, and—what was he wearing? A white button-down shirt and khaki pants...for pruning vines? Uh—*no*. Not going to work.

Jess grabbed her shopping bags—if she wasn't going to be sharing meals with Luke then a girl still had to eat—and strode over to Luke and Sbu. Luke greeted her and automatically reached out to take her bags, which she handed over gratefully. Ready meals, when bought in quantity, were quite heavy, and she was happy to sacrifice her feminine principles to get the feeling back in her hands.

'Hi, Luke.' Jess hugged Sbu, greeted the rest of the crew and then spoke. 'Good to see you, Sbu. Did you get my rough storyboard?'

'Mmm.' Sbu shoved his hands into trendy cargo pants. 'Not that it means anything, Jess. You always change stuff halfway through.'

'For the better,' Jess reminded him.

'Can't argue with that,' Sbu replied. 'Are you ready to get this show on the road?'

'Nearly. I need to put some stuff away, and Luke needs to change.'

Becca's exquisitely plucked eyebrows pulled together. 'What's wrong with his outfit?'

'Everything,' Jess replied. 'He looks like someone playing at farming, and that's not what I want. He's got to look the part and he doesn't in that outfit.'

'Thank God,' she heard Luke mutter.

'That's the most casual outfit I brought!' Becca protested.

Jess shrugged. 'Sorry, but it doesn't work. I'll be more specific in the future.' Jess looked at Luke. 'Let's dump these groceries and get you out of those clothes.'

Jess lifted her hand as Luke's mouth twitched in amusement.

'Don't even go there...' she muttered in a voice only he could hear.

'This wouldn't be happening if you'd used a model,' Luke grumbled as he followed her upstairs to his bedroom.

'I'm afraid it would. I'm obsessively detail-oriented. I'm an absolute pain in the ass to work for and a relentless perfectionist.'

'Control freak, are you?'

'Absolutely.'

'It would be fun to watch you lose control, Blondie.'

At his comment, Jess swung round and caught his eyes on her butt. He didn't make any effort to look contrite or apologetic and, damn it, she appreciated his...appreciation. Instead of feeling insulted she felt warm and feminine, and a little coy.

'Are you going to watch my butt the whole way up the stairs?' she asked.

'Absolutely...as it's in front of me it would be a crime not to,' Luke answered as they resumed climbing. 'So, are you just going to film me pruning the vines today?'

Jess explained that they were going to film him riding his dirt bike over the lands, pruning the vines and walking.

'Oh, joy,' Luke muttered sarcastically.

Jess sent him a sympathetic look over her shoulder. His eyes held a mixture of impatience and frustration and, more than either of those, a degree of insecurity that she hadn't suspected he felt. He was stepping out of his comfort zone and handing over control and he didn't like it. Jess empathised. If they'd asked her to prance around her business and smile for the camera she wouldn't be Miss Suzy Sunshine either.

She hated not being in control.

Jess stopped, put her hand on the railing and turned to look at him. For the first time since she'd met him she didn't have to tip her head to meet his eyes as she was two steps higher than him. 'Look,' she said, 'if you're uncomfortable with anything we do, just shout. Sbu and I need you to be as natural and relaxed as possible. If you're not then the camera will pick it up. So talk to me. I'll do anything I can to make this process as easy as possible for you.'

They reached the top of the stairs and Luke guided her into his bedroom. It was a good-sized room, Jess noted, with a king-sized bed. It desperately needed colour, Jess thought, being a study in neutrals. Beige curtains, cream linen on the hastily made bed... And then the painting on the wall caught her eye. It was of the vineyards of St Sylve in a swirling mist, with just the impression of buildings in the background. Jess just stared at the painting for a long time, caught up in the mystery, movement and the sheer magic of the art.

And she fell in love...with the painting and with St Sylve. It was inexplicable, but the painting smacked her in the emotional gut. She was an artist's daughter, but she'd never reacted to a piece of art as she had to this one. It was a massive canvas, nearly two metres square, but the scene was intimate and she felt as if she wanted to step into the frame.

'Jess?'

'Oh, I love that.' She eventually spoke, stepping forward to kneel on the bed and make out the signature in the bottom left corner. 'Who painted this? It's fantastic.'

'My mother.'

'You mother was an artist? My dad is an artist!' Jess told him. 'I wonder if they ever met.'

'Not likely.'

'You'd be surprised. I must ask him if he knew her.' Jess looked over her shoulder at him. He stood at the edge of his bed, his hands shoved in the pockets of his cargo pants, his eyes on the painting. 'She died when you were very young, right?'

'I was three,' Luke said in a flat voice.

Jess sat down on the edge of his big bed. 'Do you remember her at all?'

Luke took so long to answer that she thought he was ignoring her question. 'I have a vague impression of long dark hair.'

'Did you inherit any of her talent?'

'No. Did you?'

'My dad's love and appreciation for art, but not his skill.' Jess looked at the painting again. 'Do you have any more of her art? If you do, I'll buy one right now.'

'I only have this one and the one in the lounge downstairs.' Luke gestured to two closed doors on the opposite side of the room. 'My closet.'

Conversation over. Jess sighed. Damn it. He was as mysterious as his mother's painting, she thought as she crossed the room to his closet. Inscrutable and elusive and very, very compelling. Jess pulled open the doors and raised her eyebrows at the jumble.

And very messy.

There were shelves on both sides of the narrow passage that led to the *en-suite* bathroom, and the right side held a rail that was bulging with jackets and shirts. Jess itched to reorganise the jumble: there was a pile of T-shirts jammed into a space next to some files, jerseys on top of piles of paper, shoes and sports equipment in a heap on the floor.

Jess found some jeans and picked them up to find the pair he'd worn the other day—with the handprint on the seat. She turned her attention to his shirts. Flipping through them, she muttered as she pushed hangers to find what she was look-ing for...if he had it. His shirts were either too business-like or too smart-casual. She wanted something worn, but button-down—long-sleeved, but... And there it was, right at the back and half hanging off its hanger. A long-sleeved col-lared flannel shirt, missing a button and with its pocket half falling off, in a green-and-black check. Jess pulled it out and nodded. Perfect.

'Jess, that shirt is about twelve years old. I wore it when I spent a summer travelling Alaska. It's falling apart,' Luke complained when she waved it at him.

'It's exactly what I want,' Jess replied. 'Where's that hunter-green long-sleeved T-shirt and your leather belt?'

'Belt is in the bathroom. Green shirt? In a pile...' Luke grinned at her slight scowl. 'I suppose your closets are mili-tary tidy? Everything organised by type?'

And colour. But Jess didn't think she needed to tell him exactly how anal she was. 'Get changed. T-shirt underneath. This on top. Sleeves shoved up your arms. Your normal boots.'

'Yes, boss,' Luke grumbled, reaching past her to pull the T-shirt from a pile she hadn't looked in. Mostly because she'd thought it was full of rugby shirts.

God, this man needed a wife—if only to sort this mess out. Luke moved past her into the bathroom and Jess went back into his bedroom and walked over to a shelf where she could see a couple of photographs in silver frames. There was a photo of him and Kendall and Owen after a rugby match, looking much younger and splattered with mud. An-other of two elderly people standing arm in arm in the door-way of the manor. Judging by their dress, Jess surmised that they were Luke's grandparents. The man had Luke's smile. The picture in the most ornate frame was very obviously of Luke's mother, holding and gazing adoringly at, even more obviously, Luke as a toddler.

Jess picked up the frame and looked into the feminine version of Luke's face. That was what his eyes would look like if he was happy, Jess realised. They'd dance in his face… His nose was longer than his mother's, his mouth a little thinner. But those eyes, the shape of her face and that luxurious hair…that was all Luke.

Jess replaced the photo and noticed that Luke's father wasn't in any of the remaining frames. Hearing him behind her, Jess turned around and smiled. Yep, that was the look she wanted—relaxed, casual…happy in his old clothes because, hell, he *was* the Savage of St Sylve. He didn't need to dress up and pretend to be something he wasn't…

Jess smiled. 'You'll do.'

'Good, because I'm not changing again.' Luke tugged at the shirt. 'I like this shirt. I'd forgotten about it.'

Jess thought about mentioning that if he cleared the cupboard out he'd be amazed at what he found. But it wasn't her house, he wasn't her boyfriend… She changed the subject. 'Why don't you have a photo of your father up with the rest of your family?'

'Because, while he might have been my father, he wasn't my family.' Luke snapped the words off.

Whoa! And didn't *that* tell her a whole lot about their father-son relationship?

'Can we get going? I still have real work to do today,' Luke said, gesturing to the door.

Jess nodded and walked out of the room. Her family might drive her utterly insane, but she couldn't imagine not having them in her life. If Luke had lost his mother when he was three, and if his father hadn't been much of a father, as his previous statement implied, then that meant Luke had grown up without any sort of parental support system…

Jess felt her heart clench. He might have grown up on this

beautiful estate, in a house full of very old furniture, but it sounded as if he'd grown up alone. Nobody, she decided, should grow up like that.

CHAPTER FIVE

LUKE WATCHED from his lounge as Jess said goodbye to a strawberry blonde who had just deposited a massive art folder into the boot of her car. She hugged Jess before climbing into her car, and they spent another minute or two chatting before the car moved down the driveway. He saw Jess rub her arms as she turned around to head back to the manor house. Her blonde hair was tousled by the wind, and in her black jeans and short cream jacket she looked just as fresh as she had that morning—if he ignored the shadows under her eyes and the tension in her shoulders.

Luke saw her look at his front door, saw the indecision cross her face and caught the small shake of her head. She wouldn't invade his privacy, wouldn't step over the line between work and play by inviting herself in for a drink, a meal, a roll in the sack.

Luke half smiled. *Please feel free to invade my privacy,* he silently told Jess, *especially if you have more in mind.*

Jess walked over to the manor house. It was a lonely place, huge and oppressive, and he'd spent huge chunks of his life in it alone. On a cold winter's night it could be gloomy, and he didn't want Jess in the house on her own tonight.

Or maybe he didn't want to be on his own tonight, Luke thought. After a crazy day being trailed by cameras he also wanted something normal. A hot meal, a glass of wine, some company.

Before he could talk himself out of inviting Jess over, Luke walked into the hall, grabbed his jacket off the newel post and shrugged it on, and opened the front door. He grimaced at the icy wind and wondered if Jess was warm enough at night. The manor house had no central heating—his father had spent money like a Russian oil billionaire but refused to spend money to warm the house. There was a down duvet on her bed and a heater in her room, and the study had a fireplace—God, he'd forgotten to get some wood to her— but if she wanted to sit in one of the many lounges she'd need a ski-suit.

Luke hunched his shoulders up around his ears as he walked around the house and up the back stairs to the kitchen. Slipping into the room, he blew on his fingers and looked around the empty space. The kettle was on, and a teabag was in the mug next to it...

Luke stepped from the kitchen into the passageway and stood at the bottom of a second simple staircase. In the old days it had been the servants' staircase, and as a boy the only one he'd ever used.

'Hi.'

Luke looked up and saw Jess leaning on the short strip of banister on the first floor. 'Hey. I was wondering if you'd like to have supper with me.'

Jess grinned. 'What's on the menu?'

'Since you cook like a first-year uni student, you can't af-ford to be picky,' Luke told her. 'Get down here and come see.'

Jess's smile held enough energy to power a rainbow, Luke thought as she disappeared from view. Two seconds later she was at the top of the stairs and lifting her buttock onto the railing. 'Jess—no!'

Luke instinctively moved to the end of the railing and held

his breath as Jess flew down the railing and practically fell into his arms. Luke banded his arms around her and bent his knees to soften the impact of her slamming into him.

'Whoomph…' Jess muttered as they connected.

He held her as they swayed and regained their balance. Jess recovered before he did, because she flung her head back and her eyes sparkled with fun. Luke looked down at her and did what any hot-blooded man would do in the same situation. He kissed her. Hard and fast, with an already beating heart and elevated pulse. He kissed her without thought, backing her into the wall behind her, shoving his knee between her legs to widen hers, rubbing the inside of her thigh with his knee.

Oh, God, she felt amazing. Soft and supple, slim yet strong. Her perfect breasts were pressed against his chest, and he wondered if she realised that she'd tilted her hips, bringing her closer to him. Luke's hand dipped into the loose space between her back and jeans—that special area above her butt. Her skin was baby-smooth, warm, tantalising… He wondered if she still wore a thong and dipped his hand to find out. Yep, there it was…a thin cord against achingly smooth feminine skin.

Luke shifted so that he was even closer to her—so close that he could feel the thump of her heart, catch those breathy little moans as he tangled his tongue with hers. The scent of her was clean and warm, the taste of her spicy-sweet—and he decided that he'd never been this hot, this quickly.

What was it about this woman that sent him from nought to three hundred miles in six seconds flat? She wasn't the most beautiful woman he'd ever had his hands on, nor the most built. But she made him spark and then burn. He needed to have her, to taste her sweet mouth, see the brilliance of her eyes, the warmth of her smile. He wanted to see her in his bed, looking up at him, her body flushed with pleasure, legs around his waist, her eyes closing with pleasure.

He felt Jess's sigh, her breath in his mouth, felt her hands flatten against his chest...

'I want you,' he muttered against her cheekbone, and heard the rough desire in his voice.

'I know,' she whispered back. 'But it's too soon. I can't...'

'Why not?' Luke demanded, snapping his head back. 'We're two single adults, mutually attracted. Nothing changes...'

Because he was hip to hip with her, nose to nose, he felt resistance invade her muscles. And heard the reluctance in her voice. 'I've never been good at one-night stands, Luke, and we have to work together in the morning. This campaign is too important to risk messing it up because we want to scratch an itch.'

'I'll risk it,' he growled, nipping her full bottom lip with his teeth.

Jess patted his chest. 'Back up.' When he pulled away, she shook her head. 'More. Seriously—I need room to breathe.'

So did he. Luke moved away reluctantly and slumped against the wall next to her. This woman was going to be the death of him. He'd be the first person ever to die of sexual frustration.

Jess was the first to break the silence. Her voice was forced-casual when she spoke. 'So, what did you think about my descent down the banister? Seven? Eight?'

'Five. Average.' Luke grinned reluctantly. 'Not too bad. Not good, but okay.'

Jess lifted her eyebrows. 'And I suppose you're better?'

'Miles.'

'Prove it.'

Was she challenging him? To slide down the banister like a child? Luke started to roll his eyes and then he saw the dare in hers, in that arrogantly cocked eyebrow.

'You are such a chicken,' Jess said, and made a clucking sound.

He shouldn't even be tempted. It was such a childish thing to do. Jess did her clucking sound again and he glared at her. 'I take it your brothers taught you to slide down banisters?'

'Who else? We have a long staircase at home. We used to put a mattress at the bottom of the stairs…shall I drag one down from the bedroom for you?'

'I am *not* sliding down the bloody banister,' Luke growled.

Jess hooted. 'You've thought about it a couple of times. Just do it. Go big or go home.'

Luke shook his head. 'You are such a brat.'

A man could only take so much when challenged by a woman, he thought. All his life he'd run up these stairs and slid down. The last time he'd done it had been a couple of weeks before his father's death.

He squinted down at Jess, who was still silently laughing at him. 'A chicken, huh?'

'Cluck, cluck, cluck.'

'Mmm. Well, if I meet your challenge then you have to meet mine.'

'And what would that be?' Jess asked, suddenly wary.

Luke grinned. He pushed her hair off her forehead and placed his hand on her cheekbone. 'I get to kiss you.'

Jess's eyes smoked over. 'You just did,' she pointed out with a hitch in her voice.

Luke shook his head. 'Again. No holds barred.'

'It's not a good idea, Luke.'

'Cluck, cluck, cluck.' See—he could make chicken noises too.

Jess scowled at him, but he felt her acquiescence before he heard her muttered agreement. It seemed that she couldn't resist a challenge either. Then he felt the sting of her hand on his rump.

'Let's see how the master does it.'

Luke grinned, stepped away from her and jogged up the

stairs. He placed one buttock on the banister and suddenly he was ten again and flying. He let out a huge whoop as he gained speed. He was flying off the end... Oh, *hell*. At the last moment he remembered to bend his knees, and he landed awkwardly but safely.

He placed his hands on his thighs and grinned up at Jess. 'I'm out of practice. That was less than elegant.'

Jess placed a hand on his back and patted him. 'I'd say. Now, what's for supper? I'm starving.'

Jess started to walk away, and his hand shot out and snagged the pocket of her jeans. She stopped mid-stride and swore softly.

'Are you welshing on our bet?' Luke demanded, wrapping his arms around her waist and burying his face in the crook of her neck.

Jess hauled in a breath. He smelt so good—that perfect combination of man and deodorant, sexiness and skin. He spun her around, placed his hands on either side of her slender waist and pulled her towards him. He captured her yelp of surprise in his mouth and, while her mouth was open, slid into the kiss. She could feel his fingers curling into her hips, the pads of his fingers branding her through her clothes as he re-explored her mouth. She'd been thinking about this kiss—and more—for the past three weeks. Hell, for the past eight years.

It didn't disappoint. *He* didn't disappoint.

Unable, unwilling to stop, Luke threaded both his hands into her hair, tipping her head to allow him deeper access, pushing his body closer to hers. He sighed when her arms encircled his waist, the palms of her hands flat against his back under his shirt to explore those ridges of muscle, that heated skin.

She wanted him...wanted to take this kiss further, she thought as he placed tiny kisses on her cheek, her jaw, pulled the neck of her jersey down to scrape his teeth against the tendon in her neck. He feathered his fingers against her ribcage and Jess succumbed to temptation and twisted into his hand.

Luke, hearing her soft whimper, bent his legs and, placing his hands under her thighs, lifted her up.

Jess instinctively gripped his waist with her thighs, vaguely aware that he had her against the wall. She felt the icy bricks against her back when he yanked her shirt up and over her head. His eyes heated as he stared down at her breasts, covered by a lacy lilac bra.

'You're exquisite.'

Jess couldn't find any moisture in her mouth to swallow. If she wiggled she'd go off like a cracker.

'Luke…'

'What?' Luke muttered, his mouth against hers. 'Rip my clothes off? Take me now?'

She wished she could say it. Wished she could surrender to him, lose herself in his arms. But that would require her handing over a smidgeon of control, and even that would be too much. Luke had the ability to overwhelm her, and she wasn't prepared to risk feeling vulnerable…*being* vulnerable.

It took everything to drop her legs and unhook her arms from his waist. She wiggled out from under him and left him facing the wall, his forearm above his head.

'Phew! Right, where were we?'

Luke scrubbed his face with his hands. 'I have no idea. Give me a minute to get blood to my brain and I'll tell you.'

'Dinner,' Jess said brightly, picking up her shirt and pulling it on. 'You were going to make me dinner!'

'I'd rather make love to you,' Luke grumbled, turning around and tipping his head back to rest it against the wall.

Jess looked at his strong, exposed throat, the muscles bunching as he folded his arms, the frustration in his deep green eyes.

He really wanted her. To have such a man feeling so frustrated over her made her feel powerful, giddy, intensely and completely feminine...

But, as with any other drug, the high was not worth the low that followed.

Jess sat at Luke's kitchen table while he made spaghetti Bolognese for supper. The aroma of fresh herbs and garlic and the satiny-smooth slide of the red wine Luke had pressed on her made her think she was in Tuscany again. She'd adored Tuscany—the food, the wine, the old buildings and the sleepy villages.

Of course in Tuscany she wouldn't have had her laptop open in front of her or her iPad next to her. She wouldn't be prefacing dinner with talk of work. But, knowing Luke's intensive schedule, she realised that if she didn't grab his attention now she might not have it later.

And, admittedly, she'd grabbed her computer to remind them both of why she was at St Sylve. She was here to work, not play. To work, not to race down banisters like children. Work, not exchange hot, melt-your-panties kisses against a two-hundred-year-old wall...

Work, Jessica. Tangling with that mouth, playing with that delicious body was not an option.

Jess looked at her screen. The letters were out of focus and jumbled. Not only did he make her hormones jump but she also wanted to delve beneath that inscrutable façade. She kept getting glimpses of his soul, tiny flashes of resentment, sadness and more emotion than she would have credited him with. Luke Savage had unplumbed depths...

And she shouldn't be thinking of plumbing those depths, Jess told herself. Nor should she be tempted by sleeping with him either. She knew the science behind attraction, Jess reminded herself. A girl thought she was just having a simple affair but the act of intercourse released the cuddle hormone—what was it called again? Oxytocin?—and while you intended to walk away you suddenly felt this man might be the one, your mate, your destiny, the father of your children.

Then months, years, decades later you'd find him in bed testing out someone else's cuddle hormone.

All because she'd scratched an itch.

Not going to happen...mostly because she suspected that if she ever started thinking of Luke in terms of *together for ever* and *one and only* she might as well yank out her heart and ask him to stomp on it. Hard. With Grant her head and her pride had been dinged. She knew that if she allowed herself to feel anything more than friendship for Luke it would be the emotional equivalent of being disembowelled with a teaspoon. And the fastest way to get to that point? Sleep with him.

So that wasn't going to happen. She hoped.

'I can smell the smoke from all those brain cells you're burning,' Luke said mildly, swiftly dicing onions with a wicked-looking knife. 'What are thinking about?'

Jess sent him a blank look. 'What?'

'You're miles away.' Luke tossed the onions into a pan with the sizzling garlic. He nodded at her laptop. 'And you brought work...not cool since I'm trying to seduce you with my culinary talents.'

Jess leaned back in her chair and lifted her wine glass. 'You should know that my ex cooked the most amazing meals and it still took him three months to talk me into bed.'

Luke raised his eyebrows. 'Cautious, aren't you?'

'Very.' Jess held his eyes for a long moment.

It would be so easy for you to talk me into bed, but while you can easily walk away, Jess silently told him, *I'm not so practised. Sex is intimate, it's binding, and I'd be handing*

*my body to you, and some of my soul, and that scares me.
I don't want to get hurt. I really don't want to feel anything
more for you than lust-coloured friendship.*

Luke saw something in her expression—possibly craziness—and turned away without saying anything.

Jess took that as a sign to change the subject and looked
down at her screen. 'And the reason I brought work over is
that I need to talk to you about the campaign.'

'Talk,' Luke said, sounding resigned.

Jess ran through the schedule for the next couple of weeks
and told him which society events she suggested he attend
during the next month. Some were in Cape Town, some in
Franschoek, and a couple were in the surrounding wine towns
of Stellenbosch and Paarl. All were high society, and it had
been easy securing an invitation for him. Actually, most he'd
already been invited to, but he'd binned the invitations without opening them.

'Guess I'd better get my penguin suit dry-cleaned,' Luke
muttered.

Jess powered down her laptop and sat back and looked
at him. He was leaning against the counter, ankles crossed,
the foot of his wine glass resting against his arm. His eyes
were warm and relaxed and Jess felt her throat tighten. It was
such a nice end to a busy day: a man cooking her supper and
looking as if he wanted to slurp her up. Casually romantic...

Jess gave herself a sharp mental slap. If she was going to
start having romantic fantasies about Luke then she shouldn't
be in his kitchen, in his personal space.

Jess's mobile rang and the glass in her hand wobbled. Putting the glass down, she saw the call was from her eldest
brother, Nick, and she smiled. For far too many years she
hadn't received any calls from Nick, and it still gave her a
kick to see his name on her caller display.

'Hey, you,' she crooned. 'It's so good to hear from you.'

As Nick started to speak she caught Luke's frown and asked Nick to hold on. Excusing herself, she walked out of the kitchen to the hall and into Nick's living room. Another painting dominated the room—a beach scene this time, of a deserted cottage and the wild and cold Atlantic ocean. It was atmospheric, but every brushstroke seemed saturated with loneliness. Luke's mother's work…

Jess shivered and went to stand by the fire. 'Sorry, run that by me again?'

Jess slapped her mobile against her hand as she walked back into the kitchen, her thoughts a million miles away. She missed the searching look Luke sent her as she picked up her glass and drained the contents.

'Hey!' Luke protested. 'That's fifteen years old. If you're going to throw it down your throat I'll give you something cheaper.'

Jess looked at her glass and grimaced. 'Sorry.'

'Problem?' Luke nodded at her mobile. 'Bad news?'

'Not bad news. Just trying to manage my family. That was Nick, my oldest brother, being bossy and trying to arrange my life for me.'

'You don't sound particularly upset.'

Jess half smiled. 'To be honest, he's the only one I accept it from. He was out of my life for so long that it's still a bit of a thrill to have him in it. I'm prepared to forgive his managing ways. Probably not for much longer, though.'

'And the problem is…?' Luke stirred the bolognaise mixture and dashed some olive oil into a pot of water, cranking the gas high to get it to boil.

'Next weekend is a long weekend—Friday is a national holiday.'

'Yes. So?'

'My family have traditionally always spent that weekend together. All the siblings, their kids, my parents, me… We usually go away somewhere for those couple of days. I told them I couldn't make this year because I'm swamped, and because...' Jess stopped and winced.

Luke sent her a look that insisted she finish her sentence. When she didn't speak, he crossed over to her, tipped her chin so that she had to look at him and lifted his eyebrows. 'And because...?'

'Because they keep dropping hints about my ex and me getting back together. He's good friends with three of my brothers. He often spent that weekend with us.'

'But you told your family it was over? Why are they pressuring you?' Luke asked, puzzled.

'Because Grant has said that he wouldn't mind us getting back together and I was iffy about why we broke up. My brothers think I'm being temperamental and picky and just need to see what I've lost. Grant is a good guy in their eyes.' Jess shoved her hand into her hair in frustration.

'He cheated on you,' Luke said with utter certainty.

Jess's mouth fell open. When she could find words, Jess spoke again. 'How did you know that?'

Luke tapped her nose before going back to the stove. 'I saw it in your eyes. Why didn't you tell your family?'

Jess dropped into a chair and rested her elbows on the table. 'Partly pride. He made a fool of me and, as I said, they are friends. Have been for years... That makes it worse. If they find out about him cheating, something awful might happen.'

Luke stopped stirring the sauce and looked at her, surprised. 'They'd beat him up?'

Jess pulled a face. 'They wouldn't mean to. But my brothers are very protective over me. Grant will say something stupid and a fist will fly...'

'Aren't you overreacting?'

Jess took a sip of wine and looked at Luke over the rim.

'When I was five I was bullied at school. My brothers hung the bully—a girl—on a hook. All four Sherwood boys, ranging from six to ten, ended up in the principal's office.'

'Huh?'

'I was thirteen, going to my first dance. My date was threatened by the quartet. He was so scared he pulled out and I went to the dance alone. Sixteen—another boy, another kiss... Nick sprayed the boy with a hosepipe. In winter. I could go on and on.'

'Lucky you.' Luke held out the spoon for her to taste the sauce.

Jess held his wrist, blew on the sauce and tasted. It was perfect—herby, garlicky, meaty.

'Yum. Lucky? Are you mad? They are the bane of my life. They're nosy and interfering and still think I'm a little girl in need of guidance and protection.'

'But it must be nice to know that you have four people standing in your corner, ready to wade into the fire for you,' Luke said soberly, and Jess knew he was right.

Yes, her brothers annoyed her, but she wouldn't trade them for the obvious loneliness of growing up an only child.

'Or to punch an ex for you.'

'I guess.'

'He cheated. He deserves it.' Luke shrugged. 'Are you sure he cheated or was it just a suspicion?'

'I caught them in my bed. She was on top.'

'Tacky,' Luke said, tossing pasta into the rapidly boiling water. 'You're not very upset about him cheating.'

Jess shrugged. 'I'm over it. Mostly.'

'Mostly?'

Jess looked at the ceiling. How did she explain that she felt stupid rather than hurt—embarrassed that she'd never suspected he was cheating? And his parting words still stung.

'He told me I was a ball-breaker, a control-freak-psycho.

It was messy and a big failure... I don't like mess and I don't like failing.'

She didn't like being out of control, and being a perfectionist was a pain in the ass sometimes. Jess repeated the thought to Luke and he grinned.

He reached for the bottle of wine and topped up her glass while Jess draped her arm over the back of the chair. 'Anyway, to come back to my conversation with Nick... My family are desperately trying to find a villa to rent in Cape Town, so they can be near me over that long weekend. So that we can spend some time together... And my father—sorry—wants to see St Sylve. My family are wine-oholics. They've asked me to keep my ears open for a place to rent that will fit the entire family. Including Grandma,' Jess continued.

'You won't find a place to rent at such late notice. They are usually booked quite far in advance,' Luke told her as he drained the pasta.

'I know.' Jess looked glum.

Luke stared at her for a long minute and Jess frowned. 'What?'

'Being with your family is important to you, isn't it?'

'Yes. Very. My brothers alternate Christmas with us and their wives' families, so we're never all together at Christmas. This weekend is one we've kept sacrosanct. We have to have a damn good excuse to miss it, and so far my mother is not buying mine.'

Jess saw the deep breath Luke pulled in.

'Invite them to St Sylve.'

'What?'

'The manor house will sleep twelve adults upstairs and another two downstairs.'

What a perfect solution. She could have her family close and work when she could, or after they all went to sleep.

'Eleven adults. Five kids under five. Is that a serious offer?'

'It's sitting empty,' Luke pointed out as he dished up their supper.

Jess stared at the plate he'd put in front of her, her brain whirling. 'I'll only suggest it to them if we pay to hire it.'

Luke considered her words as he grated Parmesan cheese on top of her food. 'I wish St Sylve was in a position to say no, but it's not. I'll do some research tomorrow and give you a daily rate.'

Jess bit her lip and wiggled in her chair in excitement. 'Oh, I could just kiss you.'

'Feel free,' Luke quickly replied, and Jess blushed.

She would, but she suspected that would lead to more kissing.

And then her food would get cold and sticky and she was starving.

'No?' Luke filled up their wine glasses. 'Damn. Well, then, let's eat.'

CHAPTER SIX

THE NEXT DAY, Jess watched as Luke carelessly and confidently steered a hugely expensive superbike into the spot Sbu had designated and pulled off his helmet, sending a warm glance to the blonde giraffe sitting on the wall that separated the beach from the road. The sun was setting, the model had a bottle of St Sylve Merlot and two crystal glasses in her hand, and a sexy come-hither look on her very expensive face.

Jess ground her teeth. She knew she wasn't acting... nobody was *that* good. Luke strode over to the model, cupped her neck and tipped her chin up with his thumb. Their kiss was way longer than necessary, and Jess was sure she'd have no molars left by the end of this shoot. Sbu eventually cut the scene and Luke lifted his head. He really could look as if he was enjoying this a lot less, Jess thought, glaring at him as he grinned down at the giraffe.

Jess shivered and wished she had a cup of coffee in her hands. She was cold, tired, and she wanted a hot bath and to curl up in her favourite pajamas. She wanted a chick-flick and popcorn, a romance novel and chocolate... She did *not* want to accompany Luke to a wine-tasting hosted by one of the most well-respected food critics in the country.

Maybe the giraffe could go with him?

Luke was not amused when she put the suggestion to him five minutes later.

'I'd rather jump off Table Mountain than be forced to listen to her babydoll voice all night,' Luke retorted. He tipped his head to one side. 'What's your problem? You've been like a bear with a sore head all day.'

'I have not!'

'Please—your expression could curdle milk,' Luke said. 'You haven't been your normal bubbly self.'

You didn't have to watch yourself kiss her, Jess told him silently, and wrinkled her nose. So this was what true jealousy felt like. Jess twisted her lips. She didn't like it. It was so high school...

'Are you—?'

'I swear if you say it I'll swat you,' Jess warned him. 'I am *not* jealous!'

Luke grinned and his eyes danced. 'Really? Good to know. Except that wasn't what I was about to say.'

Jess desperately wanted to curl up into a little ball and whimper with embarrassment. 'What were you going to say?' she asked, forcing the words out between clenched teeth.

Luke's smile widened and Jess really wanted to slap it off his face.

'*Are you*...interested in a cup of coffee? I was going across the road to order some from that bakery over there.' Luke nodded to the bakery across the street.

Jess wanted to toss her head, blithely refuse, but she was chilled to the bone. 'Thank you.' She sent him a stiff smile.

Luke grinned, turned and walked across to the bakery. Jess wished there was a wall she could bang her head against. What was wrong with her? She didn't get jealous or snarky or grumpy...she wasn't the type. Why was she feeling possessive about Luke? They weren't dating or sleeping together, and a couple of sun-hot kisses didn't mean anything. Shouldn't mean anything...

Jealousy suggested an emotional connection which was

unacceptable on so many levels. She wasn't ready or willing to get involved again, and neither was he. They were both rational adults, in charge of their choices and their feelings. Theoretically.

Jess sighed. Maybe it was because she was spending too much time with him: familiarity breeding fondness.

Her mobile rang in her coat pocket and Jess pulled it out to see 'Mum' on the display. She greeted her mother and listened to the weekly family update. It was more rambling than usual and Jess, who knew her mother really well, wondered what her mother was up to.

When Liza finally ran out of trivia and didn't say goodbye Jess knew that she was about to be set up. Since her mother's and grandmother's choice of men was always dodgy, Jess rolled her eyes.

'He's a second cousin, spends his weekends in Franschoek. Lee. Darling, you have to remember him!' Liza pleaded after telling her that Lee was in set design in Cape Town. 'You spent a day on the beach together when you were about five!'

'Mum, I can barely remember the people I spent the day with on the beaches of Thailand, and that was last year! And, no, I'm not interested in dating.' Jess watched as Model Girl tottered across the road to help Luke carry the coffee and scowled at the warm smile he gave her. He might not like her voice, but he sure didn't mind sharing his sexy smile with her. 'Mum, just hold on.'

Jess thought for a moment. Maybe it would be a good idea to dilute Luke's overwhelming presence by spending some time with another man—give herself some distance, some perspective.

Jess could think of at least ten reasons why Luke shouldn't even blip on her radar: she was a city girl, he was a farmer. Being open and sunny herself—today, admittedly was the exception—she wasn't mad about brooding, private types.

While he occasionally mentioned his grandfather and great-grandfathers, he refused to discuss the immediate past history of St Sylve, or explain why he and his father had been at such odds. He refused to discuss his father at all.

But there was still something about him that called to her. Jess knew that she was intrigued and curious, which was more dangerous than the sexual heat she experienced around him. She could shrug off the heat but it wasn't so easy to ignore what was underneath the sexy package. His intellect, his dry humour, the well-hidden vulnerability in the tough, hard-nosed, reclusive man.

She wasn't going to be stupid enough to fall for him because, really, she wasn't a stupid girl.

The distraction of dating another man might give her some of that much-needed distance and perspective.

'Set it up, Mum.'

Jess had to grin at the shocked silence. It was the last reaction her mother had expected and it took her a minute to take it in. 'Are you pulling my leg?'

'Not this time,' Jess replied, taking the cup of coffee Luke held out. 'Give him my mobile number and get him to give me a call.'

Jess saw Luke's frown and ducked her head. *Impulsive behaviour again, Sherwood?* She didn't want to date anyone else. She wanted to date Luke. But in her mind he was undateable, and she *did* need distance.

Jess tucked her mobile back into her pocket and blew across the surface of the hot coffee. She stared out to sea, knowing that Luke was staring at her.

'You're going on a date?'

His voice was silky-smooth and she winced internally. He didn't sound happy…

Jess hedged. 'Not a *date* date. Dinner with a second cousin…it was my mother's idea.'

'You allow your mother to set you up with men?' Luke continued, in that cool, concise voice which hinted at the calm before a very big storm.

'No—yes! Look, it's just dinner with someone I used to play with!'

'Then why can't you look at me?' Luke asked, moving to stand in front of her.

He grasped her chin in his hand and forced her eyes upward. Jess's eyes slammed into his and she gasped at the emotion she saw churning within them. Need, power, annoyance...

'No.'

Jess wasn't sure whether her ears were working properly. She thought she'd heard him telling her what to do. *Nobody* told her what to do...

'Excuse me?'

'If you want to date anyone, it's going to be me. Because we both know where you and I are heading and I don't share. *Ever.* So, if you want to do the dinner-and-dating thing before we sleep together, I'm it.'

Jess, having lived with men bossing her around her entire life, didn't appreciate Luke going all Head Boy on her. 'You're delusional if you think you can tell me what I can or can't do.'

Luke's eyes were thin, very green slits. 'Try me. Don't test me on this, Jess.'

Jess tossed her head. 'And how do you think you can stop me?'

Luke grabbed the lapels on her coat with one hand and yanked her towards him. Jess held her ground and briefly wondered if she hadn't miscalculated by challenging him. She could see that he was grinding his teeth. His lips had thinned and his jaw was set.

Luke cursed and slanted his lips over hers in a kiss that was as powerful as it was sexy. She didn't go for the dominating, take-me-now type of embrace, but this was wild and crazy and more than hinted at the depths of Luke's passion. He wanted her, and he'd leave her and everybody else in the Southern Hemisphere in no doubt about that.

His arm slipped around her back and she felt the power in it as he pulled her closer up to him as his kiss deepened. Thoughts, feelings, emotions pummelled her as he took exactly what he wanted from her mouth, her kiss. Then Luke did something to her mouth that short-circuited her brain. Maybe it was the scrape of his teeth against her lip, the long slide of his tongue that had her womb melting.

Jess was thoroughly into the kiss when Luke dropped his hand and took a step back. She licked her top lip and blinked hard, trying to get her eyes to focus, felt Luke grasp her chin and eventually found the courage to meet his stormy eyes.

'Do not test me on this, Jessica,' Luke said again in a hard voice before dropping his hand and heading towards his vehicle parked on the opposite side of the road.

Jess closed her eyes and staggered over to the wall, ignoring the smirking looks of Sbu and the crew. They could think what they wanted...she just needed to get her breath back.

Breath, brain, composure... What the hell was that? She'd never been kissed like that before—an explosive mixture of furious and frustrated. Jess blew her breath into her cheeks and waited for her heart to stop galloping.

Thank goodness she was leaving for home on the red-eye flight tonight...some time away would be a good thing, she thought. That distance-and-perspective thing again.

Jess watched as Luke climbed into his car, his mobile at her ear, looking cool and collected and seemingly unaffected by their kiss. The man didn't stop working. She knew that filming took a lot of time away from St Sylve and his other business interests, but instead of whining or moaning he just made the best of the situation. He followed instructions, did what he needed to do, and in between shoots and set-ups, he jumped on his laptop or mobile to do what else needed to be done.

She knew that he was under enormous pressure, but nobody would suspect it. Luke just put one foot in front of the other and kept moving forward without fanfare and without drama. He did what he needed to do and she respected that—respected him.

D.I.S.T.A.N.C.E.

Pers...pec...tive.

She now had two mantras: *No acting on the attraction*—ha, ha! As if *that* was working—and *Keep your distance, find your perspective.*

She didn't think saying mantras was working. Stupid New Age thinking.

Three hours, a shower and a smart suit later and Luke was still annoyed. And his annoyance concealed a healthy layer of panic. Where had his caveman response to her dating someone else come from? It had been basic, automatic, primal... a reflex rather than a chosen thought...and he didn't like it. Hell, he hated it.

He'd never felt so jealous, so out of control, so plainly *ticked* as he had...did...at the thought of Jess with another man. He hadn't enjoyed the illogical reaction he'd had to the idea—hadn't appreciated the instinctive roaring in his head that had said this was *his* woman, *his* mate. Millions of years of evolution and he was still dragging his knuckles on the ground.

Maybe it was life jabbing him in the ribs? He'd been amused at the thought of Jess being a little green-eyed over the model—it had certainly stroked his ego. He hadn't once thought that he might be equally...okay, a thousand times more jealous.

Dammit to flipping hell and back.

But date someone else? He didn't think so.

Luke scowled and took a sip from his glass of '87 Merlot. Jess, dressed in a short, ruffled black dress and do-me shoes, was across the room, talking to Piers Hanson the food critic. *Flirting* with Piers Hanson the food critic… It was, Luke decided with a scowl, as natural to her as breathing.

And enough to make him go all caveman again.

There was no way he was going to watch her flirt with anyone else, he decided, even if the man was old enough to be her grandfather. Luke took a last sip of his wine, placed it on the table next to him and excused himself from the group of men around him—friends of his father who were recounting stories that he didn't want hear. *He was a great vintner, an excellent raconteur, the life and soul of the party…*

Yeah, you didn't have to live with him, dude.

Luke walked between the guests, exchanged comments but didn't get drawn into conversation. He approached Jess from behind and put a hand on her lower back, loving the feminine dip where her back met her buttocks. She knew his touch, Luke decided with satisfaction, because she instinctively stepped closer to him before remembering that they weren't talking to each other.

'Luke—Piers was just telling me that he'd love a tour of St Sylve,' Jess told him, and he saw the warning in her eyes. *Be nice, agree. He's important.*

Luke nodded. 'You're welcome at any time, of course, but it's winter and the vines are resting. St Sylve is beautiful in spring and summer.'

'I think it's stunning year-round,' Jess said fervently.

Luke heard the truth in her voice and felt warmth in his gut. He knew it had nothing to do with him. He'd often caught her looking at the buildings, touching the doorframes, staring at the mountains.

Piers tipped his bald head and his bright blue eyes were shrewd. 'You don't look like your father.'

Here it comes, Luke thought. *Another worshipper at the altar of Jed Savage.*

Be polite, Luke reminded himself.

'It's said that I look more like my mother.'

'You do. Your mother was a beautiful woman,' Piers replied and Luke felt his heart clench.

It took a lot to keep his face impassive. 'You knew my mother?'

'I did. I have two of her paintings,' Piers said. 'Such an amazing artist—and a lovely person. Threw herself away when she married your father.'

Luke's eyebrows rose at Piers's frank statement. He felt Jess's hand on his arm and was grateful for the contact. 'Uh—'

What was he supposed to say to that?

'Sorry, but unlike a lot of people in the industry I didn't like your father.' Piers shrugged thin shoulders in a dark grey suit.

Well, this was interesting. 'Why not?'

Piers looked around to check who was listening before continuing. 'I thought he was arrogant, condescending and generally a conceited ass.' He looked up at Luke and pulled a face. 'Sorry. I knew him for a long time.'

Luke's mouth kicked up. Finally, here was a man who saw Jed clearly. He wouldn't verbally agree with him—that would be disloyal—but inside he was cheering him on.

Piers sighed and shook his head. 'My late wife would be jamming her elbow into my side now, telling me to keep my mouth shut. God, I miss her.'

'How long were you married?' Jess asked, changing the subject.

'Forty-five years. Five kids.'

Wow. The mind boggled. That was what he'd wanted…one woman, one life, one marriage. Lots of kids. Now he knew that some dreams weren't supposed to come true. He didn't know how to do marriage and family—after all, he hadn't any experience of one and his father had been an anti role model.

Piers looked over Jess's shoulder and smiled. 'And here comes one of my favourite shopkeepers, purveyor of some very fine wines.'

And Luke's some-time, part-time lover.

Oh, crap on a cracker. Since Jess's arrival he hadn't given Kelly much thought—okay, any thought—and the notion that she might be at this wine-tasting hadn't even crossed his mind. They'd had an easygoing, no-hassle…*thing*…going for many months; Kelly was his go-to person when he needed a date, or sex—or even on occasion an ear. He'd meant to contact her and explain things, but with one thing and another—mainly Jess—he'd forgotten. And the thought of introducing a woman he'd recently slept with to a woman he *wanted* to sleep with made his skin prickle.

It was so Jed.

Luke, thinking that this day couldn't get any worse, quickly excused himself and stepped up to Kelly. Gripping her elbow, he steered her away from Jess.

'Kel, I—'

Kelly laid a hand on his arm and sent him a warm smile. 'Luke, sweetie, take a breath. It's all good.'

'You don't understand. I need to—'

'Call it quits?' Kelly's warm blue eyes crinkled up at him. 'Luke, when I heard via the grapevine that you had a blonde staying with you I kind of caught a clue. Honey, I'm ten years older than you. I've been expecting this for a long time. Besides, didn't we agree that we're just friends who occasionally sleep together?'

Luke shoved his hands into the pockets of his suit pants. 'Uh...okay, then. Well...'

Kelly laughed. 'You are looking very flustered. Tough day or tough girl?'

'Both. She drives me nuts.'

Kelly stepped forward and dropped a kiss on his jaw, holding her cheek against his to talk into his ear. 'Good. You deserve a girl who will drive you nuts. It makes for very interesting sex.'

If we ever get anywhere near the bedroom, Luke thought darkly as Kelly drifted back to Piers and Jess.

Piers took Kelly's hand and pulled it into the crook of his arm. 'It's so nice to see you, Kelly, and if these two lovely people don't mind, I'm going to steal you away to taste a rather nice Cab from Chile. Not as good as yours, dear boy, but palatable.'

When they'd left, Jess tipped her chin up to look at him and Luke felt like a bug under a microscope. She sipped her wine and just went on looking at him, her brown eyes wary.

'So, *that* was interesting.'

Jess's voice was so bland and so even that Luke knew she was seriously ticked. Joys of joys. Would this day never end?

He resisted the urge to tug at his collar. 'Uh...'

'How long have you been sleeping with her?'

Luke took a deep breath as he prepared to explain that he wasn't sleeping with her any more, that they were just friends, that he had no intention of resuming their arrangement.

Smart girls. Dammit, you just couldn't get anything past them.

Jess, with Ally asleep in the passenger seat, turned into the gates of St Sylve and steered her SUV down the long driveway. She'd deliberately not thought about Luke while she was away, and being insanely busy had helped. There'd been decisions to be made at work, projects to give input on, meetings to take. She'd had drinks with a potential client and dinner with another, and had returned to the office around ten to put in another couple of hours' work.

Luke and St Sylve had been put on the back burner, but now she was back and she had to deal with them. Luke had told her he wasn't sleeping with Snow White... The woman looked exactly like the popular children's character: black hair, white skin, blue eyes. Curvy. He had been, but he wasn't any more. That was all the explanation he'd given her and she admitted that it was all she was entitled to. But she wanted to know more. How long had they been together? How had they met? Had he ever loved her?

Why did she even care? It wasn't as if she had any claim on the man—she wasn't in love with him. She liked him—a lot—but she liked a lot of men... She just didn't want to have hot sex with any of them but Luke. She couldn't possibly be thinking about him as being something more, someone important...could she?

If she was, then she didn't have an IQ higher than a tree stump. She didn't want a relationship, and he certainly didn't want anything more. Did she have to draw herself a picture to explain the concept of going nowhere? Honestly...

Jess parked her car in the empty garage and switched the ignition off. Ally woke up, stretched and yawned. 'Are we here?'

'Mmm-hmm.' Jess tossed her sunglasses onto the flat surface of the dash and rubbed her eyes. 'Luke's not back yet. His car isn't here.'

Ally released her seat belt and opened the door, greeting Luke's two dogs as she hopped out. 'So where does Owen live?'

Jess rolled her eyes and pointed to the stable block. 'Luke

converted the stable block into a two-bedroom apartment for him.'

Ally squinted at the building and then back at the manor house.

Jess rolled her eyes before laughing at her friend. 'Yeah, the walk of shame won't be that long,' she teased.

Ally looked completely unabashed. She'd come to St Sylve to sleep with Owen, and the poor guy didn't stand a chance. Jess opened the back door and pulled out her suitcase and then Ally's. Ally had a very masculine way of looking at sex and men: bag 'em, tag 'em and toss them back.

Love and feelings didn't form part of the equation.

Jess still couldn't work out whether she found that sad or smart.

Jess hummed softly as she padded her way to the kitchen door. She was exhausted, and it felt as if every muscle in her body was protesting against Ally's idea of heading to a pub this evening and *'par-tay-ing'*. Jess draped her shoulder bag over the back of the chair and headed straight for the kettle, suddenly desperate for a cup of tea.

'Head up the stairs. Second room on the left. I've put you in the room next to mine,' Jess told Ally.

'How old did you say this place was?' Ally asked.

'Early eighteen hundreds.'

'Encountered any ghosts yet?'

Jess knew that Ally was pulling her leg about the fact that she believed in ghosts and wanted to see one. Like Luke, Ally was a firm non-believer.

She wrinkled her nose. 'Nothing. A house like this *should* have a ghost or two.'

'And it probably would, if ghosts existed,' Ally responded. 'Up and left?'

'Tea?' Jess asked.

'God, no,' Ally responded. 'Wine. Got any?'

'I'm currently living on a wine estate…' Jess looked around. 'Actually, I don't. Nor do I have any food. We might have to raid Luke's kitchen.'

Ally leaned against the doorframe. 'Do you do that often?'

'More than I should,' Jess admitted.

'Oh, baby girl, you have it bad,' Ally said before disappearing upstairs.

Jess poured water into a cup and poked at the teabag with her teaspoon, thinking of Luke and wondering how today's filming had gone.

She splashed a little milk into her tea and wrapped her hands around her cup, blew across the surface of the hot liquid. Hearing Luke's car pull into his spot outside the kitchen door, she put down her tea and walked to the door. Luke's smile widened as he saw her standing in the doorway and Jess felt her breath hitch.

It was frightening to realise how good it felt to be back.

Luke jumped down from his seat and, leaving the door open, took two strides to reach her. He cupped the back of her head in his large palm. His mouth covered hers in a long, slow, deep kiss that melted her organs from the inside out. Jess responded without thought, draping her arms around his neck and pressing up close to his body.

Hot, randy, slow, sexy, tender… How many ways could this man kiss? Jess held the back of his neck and thought that she could read his mood in his kisses almost as well as she could in his eyes. In this one she tasted fatigue…and a layer of stress. Happiness that she was back, relief that she was in his arms and, as always, the pulsing heat of desire. Kissing him in return, she rubbed her hand up and down his back, instinctively trying to ease the stress from his muscles, arching her own back to tell him silently that she wanted him as much as he seemed to want her, trying to tell him that she was thrilled to be back at St Sylve, with him, in the strong circle of his arms.

God, this was getting far too deep, too quickly. She should pull away, take a breath...

Luke read her mind and yanked his mouth off hers.

Jess licked her lips and tasted him there. 'What?'

Luke stepped away and put an inch of air between his thumb and index finger. 'I'm this close to yanking you into the back seat of my car and whipping your clothes off.'

Jess thought that she could go for that. It was crazy, it was wild, it was... Luke slammed the car door closed and she came back to her senses. Impossible.

She hauled in a breath and found her voice. 'Hi.'

'Hi, back. Good to see you.' Luke ran his thumb across her lips before placing his hand on her lower back and ushering her into the kitchen.

Jess wrinkled her nose when she heard her mobile ringing in her pocket. It was Lee, the five-hundredth cousin once removed, the man her mother had set her up with. They exchanged pleasantries and Jess was deeply conscious of the sardonic look in Luke's eyes. His eyes narrowed and his eyebrow lifted.

This was stupid, Jess decided. He knew and she knew that she wasn't interested in anyone else but him, so she quickly ended the conversation with Lee, declining his invitation to dinner as politely as she could. Trying to use him as a distraction was so high school and, frankly, beneath her.

She raised her brows at Luke. 'Satisfied?' she asked.

'Marginally. Take me to bed and I will be.'

Heat arced between them. She could so easily sleep with him and damn the consequences...

Owen rapped on the frame of the kitchen door and ambled inside. 'Hey, Jess, good to have you back.'

Jess returned his greeting and was amused when his eyes didn't connect with hers. He was too busy looking for Ally.

'Ally around?'

Jess grinned. 'Up the stairs and to your left.'

Owen didn't need to be told twice. His long legs took him across the kitchen in a couple of strides and then he was running up the stairs. They heard a feminine squeal, a large thump, the slam of a bedroom door…

Jess shook her head. 'You do realise that she's going to gobble him up and spit him out?'

'He won't have a problem with that.' Luke sent her a direct look. 'You ready to gobble *me* up and spit me out yet?'

He said it with such a mixture of humour and hope that Jess had to smile. 'Nope. Sorry.'

'Ah, well.'

Jess leaned back against the counter and cocked her head. 'So, how was filming today?'

'Long and tiring. I walked up and cycled down the mountain most of the morning,' Luke replied. Gloria, one of his dogs, whined at the door, and Luke looked from her to Jess. 'The dogs want their walk. Want to join us?'

Jess lifted one shoulder before nodding. 'Yes, let's do that.'

Luke lifted the heavy jacket of his she'd taken to wearing at St Sylve off the hook at the door and helped her into it. Opening the door for her, he waited for her to walk out before closing it behind them and whistling for the dogs. Two huge canine bodies shot down the driveway like bullets, tails thumping.

Luke jammed his hands into the pockets of his leather jacket, idly noticing that they had a day, maybe two more, of pruning.

Jess picked up his train of thought. 'Pruning's nearly over?'

'Yep. Time for the vines to rest and rejuvenate.'

Jess looked around her, smiled and pulled in a big breath. 'The air tastes different here.'

Luke squinted at her. 'What do you mean?'

Jess scratched her jaw. 'Back home you can taste the soot, the pollution in the air. Here I can taste fruit: the peaches and the plums, the grapes.' She turned around and walked backwards, looking at the houses in the setting sun. 'It's so beautiful, Luke. You are so lucky to own this place, to *be* this place.' When he didn't answer, Jess placed a hand on his arm and made him stop. 'You don't believe that, do you?'

Luke looked at St Sylve and then he looked away. 'No, not really.'

'Why not?'

He felt his shoulders lift towards his ears and made a conscious effort to drop them. 'I guess it's because I was never made to feel welcome here.'

Luke heard Jess's swift intake of breath and carried on walking, looking for the dogs, who'd disappeared down a bank. Jess's shoulder bumped his as she fell into step with him.

'I really hate it when you toss out statements like that and leave me hanging.'

Her grumpy tone made him smile.

'I'm a girl, and answers like that make me want to ask more questions.'

Of course they did. Luke sighed when he saw the determined glint in her eye and knew that he'd opened the door to a barrage of questions.

He'd expected a question about his father, so he was surprised by what she did ask.

'Do you love St Sylve?'

He remembered his thoughts the other day, standing in her bedroom. 'Love it, hate it, resent it... I suppose you want me to explain that too?' Luke took her hand, threaded his fingers through hers and tugged her along. 'Let's keep walking.'

Jess remained quiet, and when he'd thought about what he wanted to say he spoke. 'My father always told me that I wasn't worthy of St Sylve for a whole lot of reasons. I didn't want to be a winemaker. I couldn't wait to leave the farm—him—this valley. I didn't like my father very much and he liked me even less. But I was his only son so I inherited.'

'And?'

'And instead of inheriting an estate with normal death duties attached to it I inherited an operation that was so deeply, catastrophically in debt that I nearly lost my shirt, my skin and a couple of essential organs trying to save it.' He glanced down at her. 'Your warning eight years ago was slightly... ill-timed.'

'Now you're just being kind. I was a brat.'

'You *were* a brat.' Luke pulled her hair and wrapped his arm around her shoulder to give her a brief hug.

'So, when you say "in debt"...?'

'About-to-be-foreclosed in debt.' Luke's lips twisted. 'My father managed to rack up a debt that was three times bigger than what the estate was worth.'

Jess looked astonished. 'But...why? How...? The bank...? Why did they lend him so much money?'

Luke shrugged. 'The power of the family name—and do not underestimate the power of Jed's charm.'

'So what happened when he died?'

Luke removed his arm, stepped away from her and rammed his hands into the pockets of his jacket. 'It took every cent I'd ever made—every bit of credit I had access to—to keep the bank from taking it.' His eyes hardened. 'I don't have my father's charm. Since then, most of the money I've made on other deals has been poured into servicing the debt.'

'So there hasn't been the money to launch new marketing campaigns until now?'

'New marketing campaigns? I didn't have the money to employ a vintner. I had to learn to make wine—to do everything, really. We have a bit more breathing space now...so you don't need to worry about getting paid.'

Jess hunkered down into her coat and looked at him from beneath her long lashes. 'Can I ask you another question?' She didn't expect an answer because she carried on speaking before waiting for his reply. 'Why didn't you let it go?'

Luke looked at her, confused. 'Let what go?'

'St Sylve. When you inherited it, why didn't you just sell it and walk away? Why did you save it?'

He'd considered it. On more than one occasion he'd decided to do that...to say he wanted no part of St Sylve. But despite thinking that, feeling that, he'd never managed to take that final step to walk away from his responsibility, his heritage, his name. He couldn't allow the hard work of all his grandfathers and their grandfathers to be wasted, couldn't pass the land they'd loved into someone else's hands.

Jess remained quiet for a while after he'd explained that to her. Eventually she tucked her hand under his arm and rested her cheek against it. 'So, basically, you're telling me that a part of you loves it?'

'Sometimes,' Luke acknowledged with a faint smile.

'Well, I do. Love it,' Jess said fervently.

Luke whistled for the dogs. 'It's getting late. We should head back.'

Jess turned around with him. 'Ally is talking about getting some dinner, going to a pub later. Do you want to come with us?'

Luke thought a moment. 'Is Owen included in the invitation?'

'They'll have to come up for air and food some time.'

Jess smiled. 'So I presume so. If you don't come I'll just stay here, catch up on my own work. I don't feel like being a third wheel.'

Luke rubbed his jaw. 'Maybe we both need a break. We'll take my car. What if we leave at about half-seven?'

'That sounds good.'

'So, tell me about your trip...' Luke said as they headed back home.

CHAPTER SEVEN

'GHOSTS DO EXIST!' Jess insisted, her glass of red wine wobbling dangerously.

Luke took the glass from her hand and put it back onto the small round table they were all sitting around in Rosie's Pub and Grill. It was his—and his friends'—favourite pub to hang out in: a relaxed atmosphere, pool tables and, on the weekends, a surprisingly good band that played all their favourites.

'You know, for a shockingly smart woman, your ability to believe in nonsense amazes me,' Ally said, picking up a chip from the basket between them.

Luke agreed with her, but was old enough and wise enough not to say so with quite so much emphasis.

'Just because you can't see it or measure it doesn't mean it's nonsense,' Jess replied.

'It just means that you have a vivid imagination and no respect for science,' Ally retorted, draping her arm around Owen's neck.

His friend had that goofy look on his face that suggested that he'd been expertly and thoroughly used...and he certainly wasn't complaining.

God willing, he'd have that same look on his face before long.

When the conversation drifted to the campaign, Luke thought that he'd moved from actively loathing the process of making the advertisements to tolerating the process. He enjoyed the physical stuff—riding the Ducati, surfing, even the mountain biking today had been fun. What *wasn't* fun about hurtling down a forest trail at speed?

It was the attention he loathed. The cameras and the people constantly watching him sent him straight back to his childhood. He couldn't shake the feeling that instead of having just his father waiting for him to mess up, now he had a posse of strangers waiting for him to fail. Jess helped him get through; she had a way of calming his churning thoughts with a quick smile. Hell, just her presence and constant chatter relaxed him…although he'd never admit that to her.

Luke sipped his beer and looked at Jess. He liked her, and it had been a long time since he'd just liked a woman. Along with the liking he also respected her; it took hard work and guts to build what she had, and he admired her dedication and work ethic. Jess, he realised, was not after a free ride from any man.

Luke looked across the room towards the pool tables. 'A table is finally empty. Who wants a game?'

Owen and Ally nodded and Jess shrugged. Luke pulled her to her feet. 'You and me against Owen and Ally. That'll make it a little more interesting.'

Jess frowned. 'Why?'

'Two strong and two weak players,' Luke explained.

Jess stopped in her tracks and looked at Ally, who grinned. 'And we're the weak players?'

Luke exchanged a look with Owen. They played most Friday nights and were pretty good at pool. Actually, they were excellent. 'Uh…yes.'

Jess sent him a look that made his hair curl. 'Well, let's make this *really* interesting. Ally and me against you and Owen.'

Luke shrugged and smiled at Owen across Jess's head. How could they lose? 'Sure. What are the stakes?'

'Dinner at the only Michelin-starred restaurant in the country—the one down the road. Losers pay.'

Again, how could he lose?

When Jess sank the winning shot, she rested her hands on top of her cue and shook her head at him. Her brown eyes sparkled in the low light of the bar.

'Make the reservation, Savage, and bring your credit card with the biggest limit.'

Luke shook his head at the empty table. 'How?'

'I keep telling you that I have four elder brothers. When are you going to learn?'

Luke placed his elbow on the table and looked at Jess, who was making patterns in the condensation of her glass. She looked tired, Luke thought, and glanced at his watch. It was close to midnight and the band had switched from dance music to blues. It was freezing out, but a fire roared at one end of the room and the mood in the bar was mellow.

Owen and Ally had made their way back to St Sylve, and he supposed he needed to get Jess home, but he was reluctant to end the evening.

'Crazy week ahead,' Jess said quietly.

'Like the last couple have been a walk in the park?' Luke responded with a wry smile.

'We're filming the family scene at St Sylve on Tuesday, and my own family is coming in on Thursday night.'

He hadn't forgotten. Luke licked his bottom lip and asked the question that he'd been longing to ask since he'd heard about her family. It was one he'd frequently asked of his friends growing up, trying to capture what it felt like to be part of a group, a clan...a family.

'Tell me about your family.'

'What do you want to know?'

Luke shrugged. 'I don't know…did you go on family holidays? Did your brothers tease you? What do you remember most about your teens?'

He sounded almost wistful, Jess thought as she put her elbows on the table and cupped her face in her hands. 'Um…I felt like I was playing catch-up most of my life with my brothers. They were always bigger, stronger and faster, and they gave me no handicap because I was a girl. It was keep up or go home. They teased me incessantly and I made a point of annoying them in retaliation. Family holidays…?'

Jess thought for a moment. 'We spent most holidays at my grandfather's cottage at the beach. It was tiny, and we were packed into the house like sardines in a can. We had the best fun: hot days, warm seas, ice cream, blistered noses, beach cricket, bonfires on the sand. My brother John would play the guitar and we'd sing along—rather badly. Those holidays stopped when I was about sixteen.'

'Why?'

Pain flickered in Jess's eyes. 'My grandfather walked out on my grandmother and he and his mistress hightailed it to that cottage.'

'And that rocked your world?' Luke commented. Why would the disintegration of her grandparents' marriage affect her so much? He wanted to know. Just for tonight he wanted to know everything about her. 'Why?'

'My gran thought they had an awesome marriage. She considered him her soul mate, her best friend. Hearing that he'd been having an affair for ten years side-winded her. She moved in with us for a while, and I watched a vibrant, intelligent woman shrink in on herself. It was as if someone had removed her spine.'

Ouch, Luke thought.

'And my mom took the strain because my grandfather still wanted a relationship with her, but he'd hurt her mother so badly... It was a nasty time, and because this was *my* family, highly volatile and voluble, nothing was kept from me. My brothers went to boarding school but I stayed at home, so I heard it all: the rants, the tears, the curses.'

Luke considered her words for a moment. 'So when you caught your boyfriend in bed with someone else it was a double whammy? A visit to the past wrapped up in the present?'

Jess half smiled. 'Along with dinged pride.' She dropped her hand so that it lay beside his and curled her pinky in his. 'Did your wife cheat on you?'

Luke waited for the fist in his sternum and frowned when he didn't feel the normal punch the subject generally instigated. 'I never caught her at it.'

'Why did you divorce her?' Jess asked, the side of his hand warm against hers.

Luke stared at a point past Jess's shoulder and wondered whether or not to answer her question. Because she had a crazy shopping habit? Sure. Because she was bat-crap insane? That was a really good reason. Because...because...

'Because I looked at her one day and realised that I really didn't want her to be the mother of my children.'

'Ah.'

'Not that she had any intention of being a mother. She told me that she'd pop a kid out for me but had no intention of raising it. Since I knew exactly what it was like, being raised by a parade of nannies and au-pairs, I knew that I wanted my kids to have a mother.'

She heard the thinly disguised pain in his voice and wished she could soothe it away.

'I realised a long time ago that I wasn't cut out for the picket fence and two-point-four kids.'

Oh, Luke. You are so made to have a family. Instead of the words she wanted to say, she asked, 'Why not?'

This was the trouble with smoky bars with low lighting and cool, vibey music. Confessions and confidences tended to flow.

'I think to have a successful family you have to be part of one.'

'I don't know that I agree with you,' Jess said, moving her hand across his. 'Do you think you'd feel differently if your mother hadn't passed away when you were so young?'

Luke wondered whether he should tell her or not…after all it wasn't a secret. It wasn't talked about, but it was not a secret. For the first time in his life he actively wanted to share this information with someone…wanted her to know a little piece of his soul. Normally that would terrify him, but in this warm bar, with soft music, a couple of drinks under his belt and a gorgeous woman looking at him with tender eyes, he couldn't keep the words from spilling out. Tomorrow he might regret it…

'No, I don't think anything would've been different. My mother—a fairly moody creature, from what I hear—bailed out on me when I was three and got herself killed in a car accident a couple of days later. And my father was fickle, selfish and changed women like he changed clothes. Kids raised in a dysfunctional home do not have functional adult relationships and families. Basic psychology.'

'That's such nonsense—but back up a moment.' Jess frowned. 'Your mother *left* you?'

'She had suitcases full of clothes and personal possessions in her car when she crashed. Nothing of mine.' Luke felt the muscle tick in his jaw and closed his eyes. It had happened over thirty years ago—why did it still sting? Why did he still wonder what she'd needed, wanted from her life that had made her step out of the marriage, away from *him*?

Freedom? Another man? And would he ever stop wondering what he'd done that had made his mother leave him instead of taking him with her?

He'd been three, for goodness' sake...even *he* couldn't have been that bad.

Jess shook her head and covered his hand with both of hers. She had a look on her face that Luke had come to recognise as stubbornness. 'Who told you that she'd left you behind? And when?'

'My father...all my life.' Luke shoved his hand into his hair. 'It was his standard way of ending a conversation—*No wonder your mother left you...* Fill in the blanks. Can't catch a ball, make the swim team, come first in class.'

Jess's mouth fell open in shock, and anger sparked in her eyes. 'That's...diabolical.'

'That was my father.'

Jess's eyes flashed. 'That's child abuse.'

Luke felt sparks jump in his stomach at her defence.

'How did you manage to become so successful, so together, so strong after having that constantly fed to you?'

Because he'd been too damn stubborn and too proud to let his father win.

'And, I'm sorry. I don't believe your mother left you. I saw that photo of you and her in your bedroom—the look on her face as she looked at you. Nope, I don't buy it,' Jess said, her voice saturated with conviction. 'She loved you...there has to be another explanation.'

Luke wished there was. But his mother was long dead and, as much as he appreciated Jess taking up the cudgels on his behalf, he knew that to think about his mother was useless and self-defeating. If he considered other scenarios he risked reopening old wounds.

He'd tried marriage. It had been a failure. Losing his dream of having a family of his own had hurt a lot more than losing his wife, but he'd come to terms with the idea that St Sylve would not be home to dirty kids running wild.

Knowing his mother's motives wouldn't change that. It was in the past and he couldn't change what had happened.

'What happened to your mom's things?' Jess leaned forward, her arms on the table.

'According to my father she'd moved quite a lot of stuff out. The rest he tossed.' Luke stifled a yawn. Suddenly he felt physically and mentally exhausted. 'I remember someone saying that she took all her paintings for an upcoming exhibition. They've never been found. Somewhere, if they haven't been burnt or tossed, there are about thirty Katelyn Kirby paintings floating around.'

'Where did you find those two paintings?'

He didn't speak but Jess read the answer on his face.

'You bought them? Oh, Luke.'

At an enormous price, from a canny dealer who'd known exactly what he had.

Jess seemed immediately to understand that he'd needed a connection to her—something of hers that held something of her soul. Luke drained his glass. 'Yep.'

Jess pursed her lips. 'Dead or not, I really don't like your father, Luke.'

He saw pity flash in her eyes and his spine stiffened. Of all the things he wanted from Jess, pity wasn't one of them. He glared at her. 'Don't pity me, Sherwood.'

Jess jumped to her feet and shook her head. 'I don't pity you. I think you are one of the strongest, most together people I've ever encountered. I think you're smart and resourceful and mentally tough.' She cocked her head and listened to the music. 'I love this song—dance with me?'

Luke blinked at the change of subject and looked at the empty dance floor. 'Now?'

Jess nodded and held out her hand. 'Yeah, now. What? Are you chicken?'

Luke grinned as he took her hand and led her to the dance floor. He placed his hands on her hips and rested his chin against her temple. Moody, romantic music brushed over them and Luke's voice was threaded with laughter when he spoke. 'You remember what happened the last time you called me chicken?'

'I ended up against a wall, halfway to naked,' Jess whispered back.

Luke's heart picked up an extra beat at her soft, promise-soaked voice. 'Willing to risk that happening again?' he asked, holding his breath.

'Cluck, cluck, cluck.'

Even he didn't need more of a clue.

Luke pulled her across the dance floor towards the door, stopping briefly to throw some money on the table to cover their bill and to pick up Jess's bag. As soon as they stepped out of the bar and into the frigid air he started to kiss her, and within a minute he had her up against the building, kissing her in the shadows of the doorway. His wonderful hands burrowed beneath her coat and slipped between her jeans and the skin of her back—touching, demanding, insisting that she match her passion to his.

She wanted this, Jess told herself. She *needed* this. If she was going to do this then she had to surrender to the moment, to stop thinking and enjoy this hard-bodied, hard-eyed man who had the ability to make her skin hum. For the first time in her adult life Jess switched off her brain and surrendered herself to the physical.

His hand, warm against her, made her feel intensely female. Sensation bombarded her. The rough spikes of his beard as he dropped kisses on her jawline. His tongue wet and warm

in the dent of her collarbone. The amazing contradiction between that heat of his mouth and the icy air on her skin.

Jess couldn't stop her hands from roaming up and under
his jersey and shirt. She explored the wedge of fine hair on his
chest. She traced the ridges of his stomach muscles, groaned
at that particular patch of skin just beneath his hipbone that
was so soft, so smooth, so male. Her thumb, sneaking beneath
the waistband of his jeans, swiped over the long muscles in
his hip, exploring the wonderfulness of him.

Luke groaned and lifted his head. He rested his arm against
the wall above her head and his forehead against hers. 'I love
the way you touch me.' He cursed. 'But we can't do this here.
I want you where I can see you, taste you, enjoy every inch
of you.'

'Well, then, maybe you should take me home.'

'That sounds like an excellent plan.'

CHAPTER EIGHT

THE NEXT MORNING Jess pretended to be asleep when Luke silently slipped out of bed. Risking a peek, she saw the glorious back view of him as he headed for the *en-suite* bathroom.

So...no morning cuddle for her, obviously. Thank God.

Jess pushed herself up in the bed, pulled the sheets over her chest and leaned her head against the headboard. Damn, damn and—just for a change—damn again.

What the hell had she done?

Jess looked around the room and saw evidence of their crazy lust-filled night everywhere she looked. One of her leather boots was on top of the credenza. She couldn't see the other one. Her pink bra dangled off the lampshade. Her T-shirt was...Jess frowned and peered off the end of the bed... nowhere to be seen. Where had it gone? Jess rewound and remembered that Luke had pulled it off in the hallway, shortly after he'd started stripping her as soon as he'd pulled her through the front door. Her jeans were on the stairs—along with his shirt, shoes and jersey.

Panties? There was no point in worrying about them. They were history since Luke hadn't tried to take them off—he'd just ripped the thong apart and pulled it away.

Could anyone say 'awesome sex'?

Could anyone say 'big, huge, monstrous regret'?

Jess scrubbed her face with her hands. He'd been a fantas-

tic lover: tender, demanding, controlled, sensual and gener-
ous in turn. He'd turned her to liquid fire, inside out and...
And she couldn't do it again.

It was simply too much of an amazingly good thing. And
she wasn't remotely in control of any of it. She couldn't control her reaction to Luke's touch. He just had to look at her
with those eyes filled with passion and she was his for the
taking—battling to control the situation, the way he made
her feel...

And, damn it again, her cuddle hormone was beetling
around her body, gleefully singing, 'It *could* be a stylish marriage; he *can* afford a carriage'.

And all because she'd been idiot enough to sleep with him.
Okay, not much sleeping had happened, but she was splitting
hairs. She'd allowed those feelings of attachment a little piece
of fertile soil to take root. She'd have to dig up the bed before they took a firm hold and—what was with the garden-
ing metaphors? She didn't even garden!

Jess dropped her head. Maybe this was more than sex,
more than the scratching of a mutual itch... Because she
now felt exposed, vulnerable, scared. So very out of control.

She couldn't allow it to happen again. Sleeping with Luke
was *not* an option. If she felt this unhinged mentally and emotionally after one night, she'd be a train wreck after a week or
so. And probably fathoms deep in love with him. And, not in-
significantly, she had no intention of being that girl who was
hopelessly devoted to a guy who did not feel the same way.

'You're awake and your mental wheels are spinning.'

Look at her—all mussed and grumpy, hair a mess and
those fabulous eyebrows drawn together in an ominous scowl.
Luke thought that he'd never seen her looking lovelier...and
less accessible.

'Luke, I—'

Luke tucked in the end of the towel that rode low on his hips, walked over to the window and pulled apart the curtains. He didn't need to hear her words to know what it was that she wanted to say. It was written in neon ink all over her face. *Last night was a mistake...*

'We can't do this again.'

It didn't matter that he agreed with her. Her words still held all the sting of a powerful slap. Luke winced and placed his hands on the broad windowsill, looking out over his lands.

'Okay.'

'Is that all you're going to say?' Jess demanded, annoyance in every syllable.

Oh, *now* she wanted to discuss it? Why didn't she just put his pecker in a wringer and be done with it? 'You said we can't do it again. I agreed. Did you expect me to argue with you? Force you? Beg you?'

'No. I—I just thought that you might have an opinion...'

That it had been the best sex of his life? That he'd been mentally, emotionally blown away? That he could picture her in his bed when they were old and grey? That he knew that was impossible...?

Luke heard the rustle of bedclothes and looked over his shoulder to see Jess stalk—his mouth dried up—stark naked over to his cupboard and yank the doors open. She pulled a rugby jersey over her head and rolled the long sleeves up and over her hands. The hem of the garment skimmed her pretty knees and draped over her perfect breasts.

'Well, then, I suppose there's not much else to say,' Jess stated as she plucked her bra from the lampshade.

She bent down, briefly flashing the top of her thighs, and when she stood up a scrap of black lace fabric dangled from her finger. Her thong—which he'd destroyed with a quick twist.

'Except that you owe me a thong.'

* * *

Jess looked at Sbu and shook her head. 'I'm sorry, there's something missing.'

He was going to kill her, he really was, Luke thought as muted groans from the crew floated across the room. He caught a couple of eye-rolls from the other actors and knew exactly how they felt. They had a right to be frustrated, Luke thought. They'd been filming for the best part of the day: a mock Sunday lunch, drinking wine in front of the fire. She'd even had Luke playing chess with a father-like figure.

They were supposed to be showing him in a family/friends situation, but he knew that the entire day had been an absolute waste of everyone's time. His especially, since he was the only one in the room who wasn't being paid for his time.

'Take a break, everyone,' Jess said, and Luke walked out of the formal lounge of the manor house, where they'd been filming an after-dinner scene. Ducking into the empty study next door, he placed his hands on the back of a wingback chair and sucked in air. He knew that he was mostly responsible for the cock-up that was today. He hadn't managed to deliver the goods. He was stiff and uncomfortable and, as Sbu had pointed out, he would come across on film as being irritated and annoyed.

Mostly because he was.

They wanted to show off his home, his heritage, filled with laughing, happy people, and Luke looking relaxed and at home. Except that he wasn't. Luke walked up and down the Persian runner, its rich jewel tones perfectly complemented by the wooden floorboards. He wasn't relaxed and feeling at home because this wasn't his home. He might own it and be the last Savage, but he had no emotional connection to this house, the furniture, to the fact that his forefathers had walked these halls, to the long-ago Savage wife who had ordered this carpet.

He had the dysfunctional relationship with his father to thank for that.

It didn't help that he and Jess were barely talking. When they did, they were stiff and uptight, tiptoeing around each other. It made him feel uncomfortable and uptight and... dammit...so lonely.

You're feeling sorry for yourself, Savage. Suck it up. But acting out his childhood fantasy hurt like hell, and all that got him through was thinking of Jess and the night he'd spent in her arms. It had been a fantasy, perfection, emotionally and physically fulfilling. He'd found himself wanting to lose himself in her not only physically but mentally as well. He wanted to know her secret hopes, her biggest fears, her first memories.

Mercia, ex-wife and amateur psychologist, had once told him he had abandonment issues. Because his mother had left him and his father had never been available he wasn't able to commit emotionally, to let anyone in, to be intimate. Until the other night that had been true, and the knowledge terrified him.

He couldn't afford to feel emotionally connected to Jess... because if he did and she walked away he didn't think his heart would recover.

No, it was better this way...it *had* to be better this way.

'Luke?'

Luke lifted his head and saw Jess in the doorway, her eyebrows pulled together and her eyes radiating determination. She'd been a pain in the ass all day—demanding, precise, determined. Unbending and an utter control freak. 'We're ready for you. Sbu and I have rewritten the storyboard...'

He was done. There was no way he was going back in front of a camera and selling his perfect life. His father had done that all *his* life...acted affectionately towards him in company and treated him terribly when they were alone. He was done with it.

'Not happening, Sherwood,' Luke said in his most even tone—the one his friends recognised as deeply dangerous.

'Luke—Sbu is costing me a bomb. He charges by the hour so I'm burning money here. Can we get on with it?'

Her snotty tone had his hackles lifting. 'The cost of which will be passed to me, so don't pull that on me! I'm calling it a day, Jess, leave it at that.'

Sparks flashed in Jess's eyes. 'What is wrong with you? I have a room full of actors and equipment and crew who are all waiting on you. Let's just get it done.'

'What is wrong with *me*? What is wrong with *you*?' Luke's voice lifted. 'How could you do this to me, Jess? Is winning awards and making spectacular adverts more important to you than people's feelings?'

'What are you talking about?' Jess demanded.

She genuinely didn't know... Luke felt a knife embed itself in his chest. How could she, the woman he'd felt the closest emotional connection to ever, not realise how difficult this was for him? He walked past her and slammed the door closed.

'Luke!'

'This house! Playing happy families! It's my worst freaking nightmare. Pretending that I had one is killing me!' Luke roared. 'This was my father's office. Do you know how many times he took a belt to my backside in here?'

'I thought—'

'That corner where we were pretending to play chess? I caught him screwing my favourite au-pair there. She left the next day. I was seven and I thought that my world had come to an end.'

Jess covered her face with her hands. Luke stormed up to her and pulled them away. Tears brimmed in her eyes and they just made him angrier. He'd never told anybody this and he couldn't stop.

'The painting above the fireplace? Its frame is cracked at the corner. That's because he threw a glass at me when I was fifteen. It bounced off my cheek, cracked it, then hit the frame and cracked that. Do you want me to go on?'

'No! I'm sorry—I'm so sorry... I didn't think.'

Luke stormed away from her. 'I *knew* giving the contract to you was a mistake—I knew letting you back into my life was a mistake. I knew I was going to regret it.'

He heard Jess's sob and felt that knife slice his heart apart. He turned and looked at her, and cursed when he saw that she was shaking like a leaf. He resisted the urge to pull her into his embrace, to comfort her with his touch, to stroke away those feelings of hurt, replace the loneliness and confusion with passion...

Was that what he wanted to do to her or was it what he wanted from her?

The only thing he was certain of was that shooting was done for the day. Luke placed his hands behind his head and lowered his voice. 'Get rid of the crew, Jess, and leave me alone, okay?'

Jess nodded, turned and left. Luke, as he always had as a child, got out of his father's study as quickly as he could.

She was a horrible, horrible person, Jess thought as she pounded down the dirt road away from St Sylve. How could she have got so caught up in her job, in the campaign, and not realised the impact it would have on Luke? He'd told her a little of his father, that he didn't feel as if St Sylve was his home, but she'd been so bedazzled by the grandeur and beauty of the house and the furniture and the concept of St Sylve that she'd ignored and/or dismissed Luke's feelings.

She remembered thinking when she'd put the storyboard

together that if she got it right there would be another industry award in it for her. The setting was magical, the hero gorgeous, the story tugged at the heartstrings. At the very least
it would sell a shedload of wine...

She was embarrassed, humiliated...disgusted with herself. Awards were not worth hurting Luke for. She was such
a weasel.

Jess picked up her pace. She needed to run...run off this
churning emotion, outrun her self-anger, the confusion, his
words that were running on a never-ending loop in her head...

'I knew letting you back into my life was a mistake...'

Jess ran blindly, not sure where she was going, barely
aware that the light was fading, that black clouds were threat-
ening a deluge and that she was in an unfamiliar part of St
Sylve. The road was becoming more rocky but she pushed on,
wanting the burn of her muscles, hoping for a rush of endor-
phins that would make her feel partly human and not a complete jerk. How could she fix this? She had to fix this... He
was too important to her and she cared about him too much
to brush this under the carpet.

She'd apologise, obviously, grovel if she needed to. She'd
ask him if they could try to be friends again, make him realise that while she was occasionally thoughtless she wasn't
by nature cruel.

She had to fix this...she *had to.*

Jess yelled as her foot brushed over a rock in the road
and she went sprawling. Putting her hands in front of her,
she cried out as her palms skidded along the stones and time
slowed down. She hit the deck and her knees connected with
the hard ground. Then her right shin caught the sharp edge
of a rock and she felt her skin split open and the warmth of
blood on her leg.

It was probably no less than she deserved, Jess thought as
she rolled onto her back, grabbed her burning leg and sobbed
liked a child.

* * *

Where was she? Luke looked at his watch again. It was past six, fully dark, raining, and Jess still wasn't home. He'd come back from the lands as she was leaving for a run and he'd watched her swift pace down the road. Still annoyed, he'd headed for his study and immediately immersed himself in work. When he'd surfaced, two hours later, he'd realised that the manor house was solidly dark—which meant that Jess still wasn't home.

Luke's stomach clenched as he yanked on his jacket. Which way had she gone? Where did he start looking? Grabbing a torch from a drawer and his car keys, Luke headed towards the kitchen door and jerked it open. As he stepped out he saw the shapes of his dogs running towards him, followed by a slow-moving Jess.

Pummelled by relief, he stood under the awning over the door and leaned into the doorframe. The rain was cold and hard and Jess looked like a bedraggled rat.

'Where on earth have you been?' he shouted over the whistling wind.

'Got lost. Fell down,' Jess replied, her words almost taken by the wind.

She was soaked through, Luke thought. Her sweatshirt and running shorts were dripping and her hair was pushed back from her face. As she came into the light he noticed that she had a smudge on her chin and that her shin was dark... *Was that blood?*

Luke, unconcerned that the rain was now belting down, walked over to her and crouched down in front of her. He winced as he noticed the rip in her shin, from which blood was rolling down her leg and soaking her socks and trainers. He cursed and knelt in front of her, lifted her leg. 'Sweetheart, what the hell have you done to yourself?'

He could feel the fine tremors rippling through her leg and

heard the quiet chatter of her teeth. He didn't need to look at her to know that her face was white and her lips purple.

'I tripped and fell over a rock.'

Luke cursed again as he scooped her up and headed for his house. He carried her easily and headed straight for the stairs. Thank God his floors were wood, he thought, glancing at the wound on her shin which was still pumping blood and dripping off the end of her now red trainer. Until he cleaned it up he wouldn't know if it needed stitches or not. He hoped not. The storm sounded as if it was building up for another, even bigger session, and he'd hate to have to haul Jess to the doctor in this weather. With luck, he had a couple of butter-fly bandages that might do the trick.

Walking through his bedroom, he avoided the cream rug and walked her into the bathroom, placed her on the seat of the toilet.

She lifted her hands and gestured to her body. 'I'm so cold,' she whispered.

Luke smoothed her hair back from her face and dropped a kiss on her forehead. 'I'll get you something warm. Sit tight.'

Aware of the powerful storm raging outside, Luke flipped on the bathroom heater as he left the room. He pulled a thin cashmere jersey from a shelf in the cupboard and, tossing it onto the built-in dresser, reached for the first-aid box he kept at the top of the cupboard. The one in his car was better, but he wasn't risking the storm to get it.

Returning to the bathroom, he stripped off her wet clothes and dried her off. The pale green jersey did amazing things to her eyes, he thought as he tugged the garment over her soaked head, lifting her hair from under the jersey's rounded neck. Grabbing a gym towel from the basket, he wrapped her head in it and tossed the ends over the top of her head. Jess immediately pushed the jersey between her legs and tucked it under her thighs, shaping it over her legs until it hit mid-thigh and restored her dignity.

'Luke, I need to say something...'

Luke saw the misery in her eyes and knew that she was beating herself up for their earlier argument. God knew, he was. He'd totally lost it and he owed her an apology—but now wasn't the right time. He started to touch her chin and realised that the smudge of dirt on her chin was another graze. His heart lurched again.

'Let's park that conversation for later, sweetheart. Right now I need to patch you up.'

Jess pushed her wet hair off her forehead. 'I can do it. You don't need to...'

Luke brushed his thumb over her cheek. 'We both know that you are Superwoman, but let me do this for you, okay?'

'Okay.'

He heard her sigh of relief as the natural fabric and the heat of the bathroom eased muscles clenched from the cold. The faint hint of colour in her cheeks assured him that she was rapidly warming up, so the hot drink could wait until he'd sorted her injuries out. He had to stanch the blood, and her other leg had a graze that wasn't as serious but he imagined painful enough. Luke took her hands and opened her clenched fingers, wincing at the deep scrapes on the balls of each hand. Once the shock wore off she was going to be one sore lady.

Sitting on the cold tiles in front of her, he flipped the first-aid box open and lifted her foot onto his thigh. He patted her tense foot. 'Relax, Jess.'

'I'm not used to being looked after—especially by a man,' Jess confessed. 'My father was usually lost in his own world and he left my mother to mop up my tears, and my brothers generally told me to suck it up and stop whining.'

'And your exes? Didn't you ever get sick and need looking after?' Luke asked as he swiped away the blood with a damp washcloth.

'I never got sick and I was the one doing the looking after. I'm good at it,' Jess gabbled.

He could see shock settling into her eyes. Letting her ramble on was a good way to keep her mind off the injury.

'You're good at it too.'

'I am?'

'You do stuff for me—stuff that I don't ask you to. Even before we slept together you did things. You always made me coffee, you checked the tyre pressure on the wheels of my car. You reglued the heel on my shoe, worked out why my computer was slow.'

And it made her feel unhinged. It was interesting to realise that she wasn't used to being on the receiving end of generosity. If she was giving then she was in control...she was calling the shots.

'If you fall and hurt yourself I will mop you up,' he replied in a mild voice. 'I will check the tyres on your car if I think they are flat, because I don't want you stranded on the side of the road trying to change a tyre yourself. I reglued your shoe because the heel snapped in the kitchen and the glue was two feet away. If you have a problem, I will try to fix it. It is in my nature—hell, it's in every man's nature.' Luke flashed her a grin. 'Stop trying to control everything in the known universe, my little control freak.'

'I'm not a... Oh, hell—of course I am. Dammit, it's sore! Can I cry?'

'You can.' Luke ran his hand up her calf in a gesture that was as reassuring as it was tender. He rinsed the cloth and wiped her knees.

'Cotton wool would work better. You might not get the blood out of that cloth,' Jess said as she brushed tears off her face.

Luke looked at the cloth and shrugged. 'So? I don't have cotton wool.'

'I do. In the bathroom at the manor house.'

'I'm not going to go look for it in a storm when this is working,' Luke replied, and smothered his whistle when he saw the extent of her injury. He might just have to bandage it up and haul her to the doctor, storm or not. The cut was three inches long and deep. He could see something white and wasn't sure if it was bone or not. Blood still bubbled to the surface.

'Can I get some painkillers? Morphine? A general anaesthetic?'

'Soon,' Luke replied, distracted. The cut needed to be disinfected and closed, and the sooner the better. And sewn up...

'We have a hard choice to make, darling. This needs stitches—'

'No, it doesn't! Shove a Band-Aid on it and be done.'

'Jess, it needs stitches.' Luke drew circles on her calf with his thumbs. 'Now, I can either try to butterfly clip it closed, or we head to the doctor.'

They both looked towards the bathroom window and watched the rain hammer the pane. The wind had picked up speed and it whirled around the house.

'Butterfly clip it,' Jess told him, her jaw set.

Luke looked down and assessed the cut again. He could clip it closed. Then he'd haul her off to Dan in the morning, just to make sure. Mind made up, he patted her leg and reached for a bottle of peroxide. Past experience told him that this was the most painful part, and he decided that she might topple off the toilet when he disinfected the wound. Then he'd be sorting out head wounds and replacing a shower door. Maybe.

'Get off there and sit on the floor in front of me,' he ordered. Jess looked as if she was going to refuse, so he placed his hands on the outside of her thighs, under the jersey, and rubbed her smooth skin. 'C'mon, Jess.'

'Why?'

He kept rubbing and felt her soften beneath his hands. 'Just trust me, okay?'

'Close your eyes,' she said.

He grinned. 'Bit late, since I've already seen you naked.'

'It's not the same,' she said tartly, sinking to the floor in a move that was as graceful as it was discreet and quick. 'Damn, these tiles are cold.'

Luke averted his eyes as she rearranged the jersey again, covering up and lifting her bottom so that she sat on the jersey and not directly on the tiles. When she'd settled down, he deliberately looked towards the window and cocked his head. Her interest caught, she followed his gaze—and he swiftly poured the peroxide into the cut and winced at her piercing, pain-saturated shriek.

He could hear curses in her screams and the occasional moan interspersing her sobs. Steeling himself, he tipped the bottle over the wound again and grabbed her hands when she attempted to wipe the peroxide away.

'You sneaky son of a—' she hissed when she found her breath, tears rolling freely down her face.

Taking a swab from the box, he doused it with peroxide and swiped it over the abrasion on her other leg. Grabbing the hand that flew out to hit him, he flipped it over and ran the swab over that graze. Her towel fell off her head and her toes curled in pain. Feeling like an absolute toad, he steeled himself against her weeping and asked her for her other hand, which she'd tucked behind her back. Jess used the top of her cleaned hand to wipe away tears and violently shook her head.

'Last one, darling, and we're done.'

Jess just sobbed.

'I know it's sore, but you need to give me your hand,' Luke

told her, sighing when she held out her hand and tipped her head back to look at the ceiling. Luke added more peroxide to the swab and cleaned the wound. 'And your chin.'

Jess lifted up her chin and he dabbed it with another swab. 'Done, sweetheart.' Luke blew on her chin, dropped the swab and cupped her face in both of his hands before dropping a kiss on her nose. 'Brave girl. You okay?'

'No,' Jess muttered through her snuffles.

Taking the towel that had fallen off her head, he used the corner to mop her tears up before dropping another kiss on her forehead.

Luke sat back and pulled her foot towards him. Starting in the middle, he pinched the skin together and started taping the wound together. Working swiftly, he spared a glance at Jess's white face and told her to hold on. He wrapped a bandage over the clips and, leaving the swabs and rubbish on the bathroom floor, stood up and helped Jess to her feet. Steadying her with a hand on her shoulder, he waited until he was sure her dizziness had passed and then asked her to put her weight on the injured leg.

'Can you feel the tapes pulling?'

Jess shook her head. 'It feels tight, but okay.'

Luke lifted her up and manoeuvred his way through the dressing-room passage and lowered her onto his bed. Scrabbling in the bedside drawer, he pulled out a bottle of painkillers, handed her two and nodded to the glass of water on top of the table.

Jess looked at the pills in her hand. 'I hate pills, but I'll make an exception tonight.' Jess tossed the pills into her mouth, taking the glass of water he held out.

Luke sat on the side of the bed next to her and brushed her hair away from her eyes. 'So, what do you think we should do for the rest of the evening? Watch TV? Play chess? Have wild monkey sex?'

Jess managed a small grin at his joke. Then she yawned. 'I'm feeling so tired.'

'The adrenalin is wearing off. Take a nap,' Luke suggested as he stood up. 'Call me if you need anything.'

'Thanks.' He was nearly at the door when he heard Jess's soft voice calling him back. He walked to the bed and looked down at her, soft and small and sad.

'I can't let you go without saying sorry. I was selfish and inconsiderate...I'm so sorry. It was so wrong of me.'

Luke shoved his hand into his hair. 'And I said a lot of things I shouldn't have. Around you, stuff seems to float to the surface.'

Jess dropped her eyes. 'Sorry. Again. I'm just really sad that you regret meeting me again. I never meant to turn your world upside down.'

Luke placed his hands on either side of her and caged her in. 'Yes, you did. It's what you do—who you are. And you know that was the one thing I didn't mean—the one statement that was totally untrue. I don't for one minute regret anything to do with you.'

Jess looked up at him with enormous eyes. 'So are we friends again?'

Luke placed a soft but determined kiss on her open mouth before lifting his head. 'Probably not, but we sure are something. Get some sleep, sweetheart.'

CHAPTER NINE

JESS MANAGED TO SHOWER, get dressed and stagger downstairs. Her family were due to arrive in a few hours and she had to sort out the manor house. She wanted to air the rooms, put flowers in them, and she needed to go to town to stock up on food and drink. And morphine, and other Class A, B and C drugs, because her hands and knees throbbed continually and every step she took radiated pain into her cut.

Jess walked into the kitchen, walked around Luke, who was stacking dishes into the dishwasher, and headed for the coffee machine. He'd been wonderful last night—tender, protective, sweet. And when he'd climbed into his bed next to her he'd been careful of her all night. She remembered him forcing more painkillers down her some time during the early hours of the morning, a warm hand patting her hip when she briefly surfaced to protest against the pain.

Hearing her approach Luke turned away from the fridge and sent her a smile. 'I was just going to bring you some coffee.'

Jess pushed her hair off her face. 'Thank you for cleaning me up last night.'

'No problem.' Luke handed her a cup of coffee. 'How are you feeling?'

'Like I had a close encounter with a road.'

'That good, huh?' Luke jerked out a chair and sat down

at the kitchen table. He poured cereal into a bowl and added milk. He gestured to the box with his spoon. 'Help yourself. You're probably starving.'

Jess took the seat opposite him. She dashed muesli into her bowl. 'Not so much. But I need to eat so that I can take some more painkillers.'

'No more drugs until we get you to the doctor. You have an appointment in forty-five minutes.'

Jess waited for the familiar spurt of anger she always experienced when men told her what to do. It didn't come and she cocked her head. Strange. Maybe she was accepting his bossiness because he'd been so utterly wonderful last night.

Jess rubbed her forehead. 'Do you really think it's necessary?'

'Yes. If you don't get stitches it'll take that much longer to heal and it will scar horribly. Your legs are gorgeous, Blondie, let's try to keep them that way.'

Jess wrinkled her nose. 'It's just that my family are arriving later and I have so much to do.'

'Like what?'

'Shopping for food and wine—'

'Friends of mine own the deli on Main Street. You can phone an order in, they'll get it ready, and we'll pick it up after you see the doc. As for wine… Funny, I thought we had a cellar on the premises.'

'I can't expect you to fund my family's wine habit!' Jess protested.

'Knock the cost of the wine off my bill,' Luke suggested, and leaned back in his chair. 'Next?'

'I wanted to air the rooms in the manor, check that all the beds have linen on them, put flowers on the nightstands.'

Luke lifted his hips, pulled his mobile from his pocket, pushed buttons and held the mobile to his ear. After a quick conversation he disconnected and dropped the mobile onto the table.

'Who was that?' Jess asked.

'Greta. She used to be housekeeper at the manor. Her granddaughter Angel cleans for me to earn some spending money...she's at uni. Anyway, Greta's retired, but she'll grab Angel and get her to do what needs to be done next door. Next?'

Jess pushed her bowl away and reached for an apple. 'Want to come and work for me? I could use someone with your problem-solving abilities...'

Luke draped his arm over the back of his chair and sent her a long, slow, sexy smile. 'Why don't you come and work for *me*? I could use someone with your marketing skills on a permanent basis. Although we'd have to work on your independent, I-can-do-it, perfectionistic don't-help-me attitude.'

Jess rested her chin on her fist. 'Am I that bad?'

'Not bad. Just challenging.'

'Well, that was kind. My ex—exes—were a lot less complimentary.' Frustration crossed Jess's face. 'I was often told that I was too controlling and overbearing.'

'They sound like a bunch of—'

Jess saw Luke swallow down his rude epithet and look for a better word.

'Morons.'

'Initially they loved the fact that I was independent, then they hated it. They told me that they were into successful women, but moaned at the amount of time I needed to spend on my business. They loved me paying for stuff, but then told me that I flaunted my money in their faces.'

'And that made you start questioning yourself. Why?'

'When the romance wore off they didn't like the reality of living with me.'

'And, being a woman, you automatically think it's something you did wrong. They obviously weren't strong enough for you. And then there's male pride. None of them were as successful as you and they felt threatened by you. C'mon, Jess, that's basic psych. You know this.'

'But it doesn't matter who brings in more money. It's not important,' Jess protested.

'To you, maybe not, but to a man…? Yes, it's important! You're quite a package, Sherwood, and you need a man who is strong enough, secure enough, to allow you to fly.'

Jess wanted to ask him whether *he* was that man, whether he would hand her a pair of wings and watch her soar. Jess made herself meet his eyes and saw the regret in them.

'I'm not that man, Jess,' Luke stated quietly. 'Not because I don't think I could handle you, but because I don't want the complication of handling any woman.'

Jess forced herself to smile. 'That's okay, because didn't we decide that it was better to keep this—us—simple?'

'Yeah. But I still want to sleep with you.'

'And that is what makes it complicated.'

Luke's chair scraped across the wooden floor as he pushed it back. He walked around and put his hands on the table and her chair, to cage her in. He bent his head and his lips brushed against hers.

Jess lifted her hand to the side of his face. 'Thanks for looking after me last night.'

Luke kissed her again. 'You scared me stupid, coming back late and injured.' He pulled her up and into his arms, resting his chin on top of her head. 'Don't do it again, okay? I don't know if my heart can take it.'

Her family, in typical fashion, arrived earlier than expected, and Jess found herself opening the first of what promised to be many, many bottles of red wine at shortly after four that afternoon. Her extensive family was crowded into the main lounge of the manor house and was already settling in. Nick had made a fire, Chris was opening a packet of crisps and her two other brothers were sprawled out over the two leather couches. Anne and Heather, two of her sisters-in-law, had taken the kids for a walk, and her mother, grandmother, Clem and Kate were standing by the huge bay window, looking at the wonderful view of the mountains. Her father, bless him, was exploring the house and probably cataloguing the paintings.

'Good grief, how long before I get a glass of wine?' Grandma demanded, and Jess rolled her eyes.

'Well, if your lazy grandsons would get off their butts and help me it would be a lot quicker,' Jess grumbled.

John sat up. 'Hand over the bottle and the corkscrew, Shrimp.'

Jess wrinkled her nose at their old nickname for her and walked over to Nick, her favourite brother, who was standing next to the fire.

His grey eyes were sombre when he caught her eye. 'So, how bad was it?'

'How bad was what?'

'Your fall. You brushed it off with the folks, but you're limping and your eyes are slightly glassy.'

'I'm fine. Luke patched me up.'

'Who is Luke?' John asked as he handed her a glass of wine.

'The guy I'm doing the campaign for. He owns St Sylve.' Jess couldn't meet their eyes—especially Nick's. He was too damn perceptive and he knew her really well.

'Something cooking between you two?' he asked.

'What's cooking between whom?' Grandma demanded, and Jess groaned and glared at Nick.

'She's got ears like a bat,' John commented.

'I was just asking Jess what's going on between—' her

elbow in his ribs didn't stop Nick for one second '—her and Savage.'

'Nothing is going on!' Jess protested. Her brother and his big mouth.

'Is he why you wouldn't go on that date I set up for you?' asked her mum.

'No! I was just too busy!' Jess replied, and held up her hands. 'I want you guys to really listen to me. This is important.'

All the eyes in the room were suddenly focused on her and Jess knew that she had to choose her words carefully. 'If you get to meet Luke—and I'm not saying you will, because really we're just friends—I want you to go easy on him. He's not used to big families so I don't want you guys giving him a hard time...'

Her brothers looked at her, looked at each other, and burst out laughing. Talk about waving a red flag in front of a bull... Now Luke was firmly in their sights. She should have just played it cool. When was she going to learn?

'I wouldn't mind a friend like that.' Clem's comment floated over the masculine laughter.

Her female relatives had their noses pressed up against the glass of the window and they were not looking at the mountains. Jess prayed that the long-limbed figure walking past the window was Owen, but she knew she wouldn't be that lucky.

'Oh, my—smoking hot,' Kate said, her hand on her heart. She turned to Jess. 'Is that Luke?'

Jess nodded glumly.

'Nice ass,' Clem commented and Nick frowned.

'He's got swag...he's a real fly guy.'

Jess rolled her eyes. Her grandma had been watching MTV again.

But her mother was the absolute limit. Liza rapped on the glass and over her head Jess could see Luke turning, his eyebrows raised. Liza fumbled to open the window, and when she did introduced herself and practically browbeat Luke into coming for supper. Could she be more embarrassing?

Jess felt her face turning bright red and felt Nick's not-so-gentle elbow in her ribs.

'So, just a friend, huh? You sure about that?'

Jess heaved in some air and thought that it was going to be a very long weekend indeed.

He'd planned to keep his distance from Jess while her family were visiting, but that first evening he'd somehow found himself seated at the head of the two hundred-year-old dining table that had been brought out by one of the early Savage wives at the beginning of the nineteenth century. The Sherwood clan occupied the rest of the table…and, Lord, what a clan they were.

Loud, noisy, charming…loud, noisy. Well, all except for Nick, the oldest brother, who observed more than he partook in the conversation, a wry smile on his face. Of all of Jess's brothers this was the one he liked most…possibly because he didn't seem as if he was operating at warp speed.

He had to admit that Jess's brothers had spectacular taste in women…from Nick's fiancée, Clem—a stunning redhead and once-famous model, the ex-girlfriend of rocker Cai Clouston—to the other wives. Two brunettes and a blonde, they were all lookers. All educated and independent. One was an ex-teacher turned columnist, one a doctor and one a physiotherapist. The Sherwood brothers liked brains with their looks.

Just like he did.

Luke looked at Jess, deep in conversation with her father. Their brown eyes were identical. He'd have to be blind not to notice the speculative looks they'd sent his way, the not-so-subtle questions about their relationship. He'd ducked them all. He figured it was up to Jess to explain their relationship, and that she would be returning with him to his house tonight.

He just wished he could say, even if it was only to himself, that she would be sleeping in his bed with him again.

She was…beautiful, Luke thought, looking at her. Her hair was messy, her lipstick was long gone, and she had shadows under her eyes from pain—ten stitches, and she'd thought she didn't need to see a doctor!—but she glowed.

She loved her family, loved being around them, he realised. He'd watched their arrival from his lounge window and had heard her squeal when she'd seen the convoy of cars turning into St Sylve. The cars had barely stopped before she'd wrenched doors open and children and toddlers had clamoured for kisses and hugs from her. He'd gritted his teeth when one brother had swung her around—*stitches, dammit!*—before passing her like a pretty parcel to the next brother, who'd repeated the process.

Luke shook his head. Jess had never, not for one moment, doubted that she was loved…

This was the type of family he'd have sold his soul for as a child and teenager. If he could have ordered it this was what it would have looked like. Siblings, laughter, teasing, loud conversation.

'Quiet down, everyone…'

Luke turned his attention to Jess's dad as the conversation died down. David Sherwood lifted his wine glass. 'I'd like to thank Luke for opening up his house to our craziness, and fervently hope he doesn't regret it.' David narrowed his eyes and they bounced from one child to another. Jess, Luke noticed, wasn't left out. 'And that means no rough-housing amongst the furniture, no sliding down banisters, no flour bombs from the upstairs windows.'

Luke leaned towards Nick, who was sitting to his right. 'He's talking to the kids, right?'

Nick's grey eyes laughed. 'Unfortunately, no. My brothers and my sister can be quite wild on occasion.'

Luke grinned. 'And you're not?'

'I just don't get caught,' Nick replied with a chuckle.

'Anyway, thank you, Luke, for allowing us to be together this weekend.' David lifted his glass and when the cheers died down continued to speak. 'By the way, I knew your mother.'

Luke saw Jess's hand jerk her father's arm and he caught her eye. Sending her a reassuring glance and the slightest shake of his head, he silently told her that he wanted to hear about his mother. God, he knew nothing about her—of course he wanted to hear about her.

'Really? How did you know her?' Luke was quite impressed that his voice sounded vaguely normal.

'We went to art school together in Cape Town. I think I was half in love with Katelyn.'

'You were half in love with everyone at uni,' his wife said crisply. 'Katelyn...Katelyn Kirby? I remember her. Long hair, green, green eyes. *Your* eyes.' Liza leaned across Nick to touch his hand quickly with the tips of her fingers. 'I'm sorry you lost her so young, Luke.'

Such simple, sincere words. It almost made him want to tell her that he hadn't lost her, she'd already gone...

'I remember going to her older sister's cottage, near Lambert's Bay. The sister raised her—she was a professor of archaeology at UCT, often away on digs.'

David took a sip of wine and Luke swallowed. God, he had an aunt. How...? Why...? He'd never known he had an aunt.

Not that it mattered after so much time, he had no intention of tracking her down but...*wow*, he had an aunt.

'I loved her work. Adored her work,' David rambled on. 'She was destined for great things. Then there was Greg Prescott...'

'And Dad's off and running,' Nick muttered. 'Heaven help

us. He's going to give us a dissertation on every artist he ever knew.'

'Distract him—quick!' Luke heard another brother—John— hiss.

Patrick jumped in and spoke over his father. 'So, when are we going to settle our bet, Shrimp?'

Luke's head snapped up. Bet? What bet?

'We have time this weekend. We can find a five-kilometre route and settle this once and for all,' Patrick goaded Jess.

'Oh, goodie.' Liza clapped her hands. 'I'm sick of dripping taps.'

Luke saw Jess wince. What was going on?

When Jess didn't speak, Patrick leaned across the table and got in her face. 'Chicken, Jess? Are you being a girl?'

'I *am* a girl, frog-face.'

Luke saw stubbornness creep into her expression. He looked at Nick again. 'Want to explain what the bet is?'

'Who can run a quicker five-k.'

'Me,' Jess and Patrick chimed in unison.

Luke poured wine into his glass and took a sip before pinning Jess with a look. 'No.' He saw the protest start to form on her lips and knew that her instinctive reaction was to baulk. 'Not negotiable, sweetheart,' he added in his firmest voice.

Jess held his glare for a long minute before muttering mutinously, 'I'll be fine.'

'Ten.' Luke held up both his hands. He knew that she didn't want her family to know that she'd had stitches in her leg, that she didn't want them fussing over her—especially the two doctors—so he'd agreed to keep her secret. But not if she was thinking about racing her brother over five kilometres.

He saw Jess's lips move in a silent curse and hid his smile when she finally looked at Patrick. 'Not this weekend, slowpoke. I'm still a bit sore from my fall.'

Patrick seemed to accept that as a valid excuse, Luke

thought, feeling Nick's interested gaze on his face. He turned his head and lifted his eyebrows. 'What?'

'Well, that was interesting. Ten what?'

Luke ignored him, but Nick wasn't the only brother to have picked up on the tension between him and Jess. Patrick geared up to needle his sister again.

'So what's the deal between you and Savage, Jess? I think that's the first time in history that you've listened to a man without an argument.'

Jess leaned across the table and skewered him with a hot look. 'What's the deal between you and brains, Pat? As in... where are yours? And mind your own business.'

'You *are* my business. Our business.' Patrick spooned up his dessert and leaned back in his chair.

Nick rolled his eyes. 'Here we go.' He turned to Luke. 'Patrick and Jess have butted heads their entire lives. They are only nine months apart, and Pat loves to lord it over her. Not that we're not *all* interested in what's happening between you and our baby sister.'

'But you're just quieter about it?' Luke shot back, and read the warning in Nick's eyes. *Mess with her and you're a dead man.* Which annoyed him... After all, she hadn't caught *him* in bed with someone else.

And never would. He didn't cheat.

'I counted the bedrooms and there's just enough for all of us,' John commented. 'So, where are you sleeping, Jessica?'

Every single Sherwood, plus wives and partners, perked up. Her mother leaned forward in her chair. Her grandmother chuckled. Faces turned either speculative or protective and Jess threw Luke a desperate look.

Ah...this was the downside of a large family. The extreme lack of privacy. 'I offered Jess a place to sleep in my house for the duration of your stay. Since we do need to do some work this weekend, we thought that was the most practical solution.'

'So are you sleeping together, and if you aren't, why not?' Liza raised her eyebrows. Liza didn't give him a millisecond to respond. 'Are you involved? Married? Gay?'

'Mum!' Jess shoved her hands into her hair from frustration.

'What?' Liza sent her an innocent look. 'I just want you to be happy. And if you and Luke are just work colleagues then I have at least three young men who want your number.'

'Good grief,' Jess moaned. 'I told you—Luke and I are friends. Just friends.'

'Then maybe you and Grant can get back together?' Patrick suggested. 'I saw him last week. He was asking about you.'

A chorus of approval followed his suggestion and Luke felt his teeth grinding in the back of his jaw.

'He isn't seeing anyone else,' Chris commented. 'We took him out for a beer and he was crying into it, saying that you were the best thing that ever happened to him. Can't understand it myself, but there you are.'

'He's a nice guy, Jess,' John agreed.

Jess sent Luke a look of abject misery and mortification. He now knew what she'd meant when she'd said that her family didn't respect her privacy and that they had no concept of emotional boundaries.

Patrick waved his wine glass in the air. 'And he's a mean fly half. If he's prepared to forgive her for being so anal then she should consider giving him another chance.'

Clem shook her head at Kate. 'For a doctor, your husband can be extraordinarily thick on occasion.'

'Tell me about it,' Kate grumbled.

Jess pushed her chair back and stumbled to her feet. Luke saw the white ring of pain around her mouth and knew that she was at her limit—physically and probably mentally—and certainly not up to dealing with her family. When she swayed on her feet his protective streak flashed white-hot, and he was out of his chair to catch her as her knees buckled. He'd been wrong. She was way past her limit.

'Okay, that's enough,' he said in a hard voice.

Luke wound his arm around her waist and felt Jess's arms creep around him. He looked at each of her brothers in turn.

'God, you lot are a piece of work. Can't you see that she's not up to dealing with your crap? She's got ten stitches in her leg and she's battered and bruised.'

His glare had Patrick's retort dying on his lips.

'Jess and I—hell, I don't even know what's what between us. But—' he looked at Liza '—it is *between us*. And the next person who mentions her going back to that waste of oxygen she caught screwing another woman, in *her* bed, will get his ass kicked. By me.' Luke lifted his hand to cradle Jess's head against his chest. 'I am taking Jess home. She's had more than enough. She'll see you in the morning—if she's feeling up to it.'

Luke guided Jess out of the room and a silent Sherwood family watched them leave.

Nick broke the shocked silence that followed. 'Well, well, well. Jess has finally found a man who has a bigger set than she does. Good for her and it's about time. Pass that wine, Grandma, you're hogging it.'

For the second night in a row Jess slept in Luke's bed—in the proper sense of the word. There had been no euphemisms involved because shortly after carrying her up the stairs he'd handed her some painkillers and bustled her into bed. Her head had barely hit the pillow and she was asleep.

Sexy she was not.

Jess rolled over as she smelt coffee and swallowed saliva as Luke walked into the room, dressed in nothing more than a low-slung towel over his slim hips. Lord, he had a beautiful body...

He smiled down at her as he put the cup of coffee on the bedside table. Jess sat up and squinted at the clock. It was just past nine—an unusual time for Luke to be showering.

'When I came back from the lands your brothers were about to go for a run and invited me to join them,' Luke explained, sitting on the bed next to her. 'Obviously it was a test. Competitive bunch, aren't they?'

Jess groaned. 'Sorry. Did they go all he-man on you?'

'Well, they did try to outpace me.' Luke smiled into his coffee cup. 'I managed to keep up.'

Jess took her cup and winced when her injuries brushed the bedclothes. 'If you beat Patrick I'll kiss you senseless.'

'I beat Patrick. I ran twenty-three-ten.'

Jess's jaw dropped open. 'You beat them all?'

Luke looked like the cat who ate the cream. 'I *whipped* them all.'

'Woo-hoo!' Jess shouted with glee. 'You are the *man*!'

Jess settled back on the pillows and after a minute or so smiled at Luke. 'You know that you're going to have to marry me now, don't you?'

Luke spluttered tiny drops of coffee over his white towel. 'What?'

Jess patted his knee. 'By standing up for me last night, you—in my mother's eyes at least—practically declared your intentions. As I speak, she's probably planning our wedding.'

'God, families are complicated,' Luke complained. 'And yours is, I suspect, more complicated than most.'

'I'm the youngest child—a daughter with four older protective brothers.'

'Who threatened to cut off my balls if I hurt you,' Luke told her.

'Oh, grief, they didn't?' Jess blew air into her cheeks. 'Of course they did… Sorry. Did they thump their chests as well?'

Luke grinned. 'Yep. Then they spent the rest of the run

deciding what to do about your ex. Concrete shoes were mentioned.'

'Their anger will blow off and then they'll just ignore him. I hope.' Jess sipped her coffee. 'I'm sorry. I know that they are impossible and in-your-face. I'll understand if you want to keep your distance from them…'

Luke placed his hand on the other side of her stretched out legs and leaned on it. 'I haven't had much to do with large families, Jess—hell, with *any* families. I don't know how to act, what to do… Last night I was nervous as anything.'

'Seriously? You didn't look it.'

'Practice. My legs were bouncing under the table.'

Jess heard the insecurity in his voice and felt her heart jump into her throat. 'You just need to be who you are, do what you do. Don't worry about my mother and her machinations. If your little speech last night didn't get through to her, she knows that I can't and won't be forced into anything. So, what do you think about the fact that my dad knew your mom?'

Jess felt his mood shift from relaxed to wary.

'I guess the art world in the seventies was smaller than I supposed.'

'Are you going to try to track down your aunt?'

Luke lifted his head to look at her. 'Why should I?'

Why should he? Jess frowned. 'Luke, she could tell you about your mother.'

Luke's face hardened. 'I know all I need to about Katelyn. She was a really good artist who decided she didn't want me any more. Then she died.'

The lack of emotion in his voice whipped at Jess's soul. It spoke of hurt and betrayal buried deep. 'Your aunt could explain—'

'I'm thirty-six years old. She must've known about me.

She's had thirty-plus years to find me and explain,' Luke shot back. 'It's not like we went anywhere.'

His tone told her to leave the subject alone and Jess backed off. They'd just got back onto an even keel. She didn't want to argue with him and risk upsetting that.

Muscles rippled in Luke's torso as he leaned forward and gently touched her chin with the tips of his fingers. 'How are you feeling?'

Jess licked her lips at the passion slumbering in his eyes. 'Good. Much better.'

Luke moved forward and slipped his hand around her neck. 'Then did I hear you say something about kissing me sense-less? Especially since I whipped your brothers?'

'I might have said that,' Jess whispered as his head dropped. She sighed when his lips met hers in a kiss that was as simple as it was devastating. She wanted more than just a kiss. She wanted him in every way.

Luke's tongue tangled with hers and she reached out her hand and patted his waist, finding the towel and tugging.

Luke pulled back and sent her a look full of regret and frustration. 'Sweetheart, we can't. Your leg.'

Jess tugged again. 'You'll be careful of me. I trust you,' she said against his mouth. 'I'm tired of just sleeping in your bed, Savage.'

Luke covered her as his towel fell open. 'Well, when you put it like that…'

CHAPTER TEN

JESS STOOD at the kitchen sink in the manor house, washing dishes and watching Luke, Owen and Kendall taking her brothers on at touch rugby on the swathe of lawn just beyond the window. Luke looked happy, Jess thought. He was dirty and sweaty, but laughing at the creative insults her brothers traded on a regular basis.

Jess felt a feminine hand on her back and smiled at Clem. 'Hi.'

'Hi, back. Why are you hiding out in the kitchen?'

Jess lifted one shoulder. 'I needed a break.' She looked at Nick's partner and said a quiet thank-you to Nick for bringing such a wonderful woman into their family, her life. She adored her sisters-in-law but, despite not knowing Clem for very long, felt closest to the ex-model and socialite.

'Are you okay, Jess?'

Jess pushed her hair off her forehead with the back of her wrist and shrugged. 'Yes…no…confused.'

'Luke?'

'Who else?' Jess looked out of the window. 'He's got baggage, Clem…'

'Don't we all, sweetie? You have a frequently impossible family and a strong independent streak. I had no idea who I was or what I wanted before I met Nick. I was the ultimate spoilt princess.' Clem leaned her bottom against the counter next to Jess and crossed her long, slim legs. 'None of us is perfect, Jess-jess.'

'And he doesn't want a relationship. What did he say to me…? He doesn't want to have to "handle" any woman.'

'Ouch. And do you want a relationship with him?'

'Kind of.' Jess gave Clem a rueful smile. 'I've fallen in love with him. When Luke stood up for me to my brothers last night I knew that he was the man for me.'

'Yeah, I realised that too. He's strong enough, secure enough, smart enough—perfect for you.'

Clem just *got* it. Jess didn't need to explain that she felt Luke was the flipside of her coin. Strong enough to lean on, masculine enough for her to enjoy, even flaunt her femininity, with enough tenderness to balance out his machismo.

This was what love felt like, Jess realised. Like a multi-layered, delightful cake, each layer rewarding in its own right. Attraction that ignited a low hum in her womb whenever he looked at her, a touch that chased sexual shivers up her spine, a dry sense of humour and a sneaky intelligence that kept her off guard.

He was her perfect fit—except…

'Except he isn't interested. Not in permanence, commitment, marriage or any possible combination or permutation of the above.' Wasn't it just so typical that when she finally found someone she was prepared to fall in love with he was unavailable and uninterested?

Clem rubbed her shoulder with her hand in a gesture that was as sweet as it was comforting. Jess told Clem about the disastrous shoot earlier in the week and her part in it.

'I really wanted a family scene, but I can't—won't—put Luke through that again.'

Clem looked at her for a long minute, held up a finger and walked away. Within a couple of minutes she was back, a hand-held camcorder in her hand. Clem nodded to the window and handed Jess the camcorder. 'There's your family scene, Jess. Film it.'

Jess looked out and saw what Clem was getting at. There were the Sherwood wives—gorgeous and relaxed, wine glasses in hand, talking furiously—sitting on a patch of grass to the side of the mock rugby pitch. Jess lifted the camera and zoomed in, then tracked the outline of the manor house onto the veranda, where her father sat in an easy chair, a sketch-pad and John's three-year-old on his lap, directing his hand as he drew. Liza had a sleeping baby in her arms and was watching the rugby.

Jess panned the camera over the table between them: St Sylve wine bottles and half-filled glasses, an open book lying face-down, a baby's pacifier, a colouring book and crayons, a half-empty bowl of the apple crumble they'd had for pudding...

Jess went to Luke, hands on his thighs, his face turned away. He looked happy, she thought, relaxed—as she'd wanted to catch him the other day. Enjoying himself, having fun.

Jess carried on filming and her mouth curved into a delighted smile. 'You, Clem Campbell, are a genius.'

Clem looked at her nails and smiled. 'I know, but feel free to remind Nick.'

Luke followed the massive Sherwood clan to their hired cars and hung back as Jess kissed and hugged her family goodbye. The days had passed quickly, and Luke realised that he'd had more fun than he'd had in ages with her family. He hadn't had much time to himself or with Jess, and neither of them had got any work done, but he was okay with that. He felt as if he'd had a mini-holiday without leaving his house.

He'd taken them all over the farm, explained the wine-making process to her father and brothers, discussed the history of the property with Jess's mother and grandmother. He'd exercised with her brothers in the gym, been sketched by her father, taken the kids for rides on his dirt bike and tractor.

And now he was being thanked and hugged and kissed. Luke bent down so that Jess's tiny grandmother could kiss him goodbye, and then turned to shake her father's hand.

'Thank you for your hospitality, Luke,' David said. 'Look after my girl.'

'It's not like that…' Luke replied, feeling a cord tighten around his neck.

David's warm brown eyes laughed at him. 'Yeah, right.'

Liz elbowed her husband out of the way and tucked a piece of paper into Luke's shirt pocket and patted it. 'The name of your aunt and her address. I have an old university friend who had the details. Go talk to her.'

Uh, no. Thank you anyway.

'Take care of my baby.' Liza kissed him on one cheek and then the other.

The cord tightened. He had a break when the wives kissed and hugged him, and then there were the brothers, standing in one solid line, identical scowls on their faces. He looked around for Jess but she'd run back into the house to fetch a book her grandmother had left behind.

John pulled out a folded piece of paper from his back pocket and slowly opened it. 'As the oldest, it behooves me—'

'Behooves?' Patrick snorted.

'Shut up, squirt. It behooves me to establish whether you are worthy of Jess.'

Luke rolled his eyes. Really? Were they *really* going to pull this?

'Super 14 Rugby. Who do you support?'

'Really? This is what is important?' Luke felt insulted on Jess's behalf.

John ploughed on. 'Man United or Chelsea?'

'Liverpool,' Luke replied, just to be facetious.

'Do you drink and drive?'

No.

'Are you an aggressive drunk?'

No again.

'Do you cook?'

Yes, thank God, since Jess had the cooking skills of a tortoise.

'Do you understand the African tradition of lobola?'

Huh? What?

Luke frowned and Nick grinned. 'You know—paying the family for the honour of their daughter's hand in marriage?'

He looked across at David, who just smiled and shrugged. 'They negotiate for me.'

Luke folded his arms and kept quiet, scowling fiercely. Good God, what had he done so wrong in his life, or in a previous life, that warranted this?

'We want fifteen cases of that outstanding Merlot 2005, use of the manor house for family holidays, and Dad wants a breeding pair of silky bantam chickens,' John explained.

Luke threw up his hands. 'Chickens? You've got to be kidding me!'

'I wanted goats, but Liza put her foot down,' David replied.

'Good grief,' Luke said faintly, and rubbed the back of his neck. 'Listen, I hope this is your sick idea of a joke, because this is the most absurd conversation. I am not—*we* are not—talking or thinking about marriage. I don't want to get married!'

Chris grinned. 'None of us did, dude! But here we all are…'

Jess darted out of the house, book in hand, and immediately, Luke noticed, her brothers feigned innocence.

John gripped his hand and squeezed. Hard. 'You hurt her, you answer to us.'

Luke wished he could brush off his words as chest-thumping, but he knew they were deadly serious. If he messed Jess around he would be fish food. He shook Chris's and Patrick's hands, lost the feeling in his fingers again and resisted the impulse to nurse it before turning to Nick.

He scowled at Jess's favourite brother. 'Yeah, yeah...I get it. Don't mess with Jess.'

Nick shook his head and put his arm around Clem's waist. 'I was just going to wish you luck. You're going to need it, dealing with that brat.'

'Thank you,' Luke replied fervently. At least someone was on his side.

Nick slapped him on the shoulder before shaking—squeezing, *ow*, dammit!—his hand. 'But she sheds one tear over you and I'll stake you to an anthill.'

Nice, Luke thought.

He watched the cars disappear down the drive and looked at Jess, whose eyes were fixed on the backs of the vehicles. He caught the expression crossing her face as she jammed her hands into the front pockets of her jeans and watched them leave...a little sadness, a little relief. She was a strong, independent woman, but her family were her rock, he realised, her north star, the wind that helped her fly. While they occasionally irritated and frustrated her, she adored them, and she also missed them...

Being here, with him, at St Sylve, deprived her of them. It was just another reason in a long list of reasons why they could never be together long-term. She needed that family atmosphere and he couldn't—wouldn't—provide it for her.

Besides, even if they wanted to continue their...whatever it was, how would it work? Practically? Logistically? His life was here on St Sylve. Hers was across the country. She had a successful business based in another city—one that she'd sweated blood and tears to establish. He couldn't imagine giving up St Sylve, so he knew that to ask her to give up Jess Sherwood Concepts would be deeply unfair.

What was he going to do about her? He'd never intended to become involved with a woman again, but Jess, being Jess, had become more than a fling, more than a quick and casual affair. He couldn't allow himself to get any more attached to her than he already was. It would be easier to have open-heart surgery without anaesthetic than to risk loving someone and having them leave him.

Luke felt the sour taste of panic in the back of his throat and pulled at his shirt collar. He'd been living in a dream world these past few days and it was time to snap out of it. He'd been seduced—literally and metaphorically—by the woman in his bed and her family in the manor house.

It wasn't real and it sure wasn't permanent.

Nothing ever was.

'So, how is Luke?'

Jess sat at a small wooden table at a restaurant in Lambert's Bay, a cup of coffee in front of her, waiting to meet Luke's cousin. She was talking to Clem, all the way across the country at their safari operation, Two-B.

'Distant, irritable, moody and snappy.'

'Oh. Um…that's not what I expected to hear. I thought you would be burning up the sheets.'

'We are,' Jess replied. 'We're just not talking in between. We both know that I should be packing to leave but neither of us are mentioning it.'

When he was making love to her he was anything but broody and snappy. Passionate, loving, attentive, tender. His body worshipped hers…

'Have you asked him about it?'

'Mmm, a couple of times. Yesterday I asked why he was being so aloof, far-away…uncommunicative, and was told that he has a lot of his mind. That he's working on a couple of difficult deals and he's tired.'

Clem was silent for a moment. 'Is he back-pedalling?'

Jess rested her forehead on her fist and nodded, then re-alised that Clem couldn't see her.

'I think that's part of it. I also think he's thinking about his mum a lot. I think it's natural after being confronted with our family.'

She really believed that. When she'd caught Luke staring at the photograph of his mum this morning all the pieces had fallen into place. Spending so much time with her family, see-ing how close they were, had to make him wonder about his own family—about the fact that he had an aunt. He would be wondering whether he had cousins, other family members he'd never met. So she'd raised the subject of Luke tracking down his aunt again and he'd brushed her off. She realised that his reaction was a combination of fear and bravado, and understood that he was anxious. Who wouldn't be? But he wasn't uninterested so that was why...

'I'm in Lambert's Bay, about to meet his cousin,' Jess said. She'd found the slip of paper her mum had given Luke, di-alled the number of the cottage and spoken to Luke's cousin. Luke's aunt had died a couple of years ago, she'd explained, but she'd grown up with the tragic tale of Katelyn and would be happy to share the story with Jess—especially if she was living with Luke. Well, it wasn't a lie...she *was* living with Luke. She just hadn't felt the need to tell her that it was a temporary arrangement.

'Does he know?'

'No.'

'Do you think that's wise?'

'It's my gift to him, Clem. Knowledge about his past, his mother.'

It was her way to show him how much she loved him, that

she would love to make a family with him, to invite him to share hers. Like her brothers, she wanted to love and be loved, to create her own family within a bigger one.

'I want a man who loves me like Nick loves you—like Dad still loves my mum.'

'Oh, sweetie, I hear you. But I'm not sure if this is the right way to go about it,' Clem said. 'Changing the subject—how did the family advert turn out?'

'Sbu and I did the final edit on it this afternoon. It's wonderful—funny, warm and very accessible. Everything I wanted it to be. I just need to show it to Luke and get his approval to flight the ad and we're done, business-wise.'

'Meaning that you should be heading home?'

Jess felt her stomach sink. She didn't want to leave him—didn't want to go back to her empty life in Sandton. She wanted to stay at St Sylve... She had thought this through: if Luke asked her to stay she'd open another branch of Jess Sherwood Concepts in Cape Town, leaving Ally to run the Sandton branch.

She could have a remote office at St Sylve...what was the point of wonderful technology like video conferencing and e-mail if one didn't use it?

She'd miss her family, but being with Luke was non-negotiable.

'I don't know how I am going to leave him, Clem. If he doesn't ask me to stay it's going to break my heart...'

Jess looked up as the door to the coffee shop chimed and a tall woman her own age walked through the door. The first of Luke's family...she couldn't wait to meet the rest.

'I've got to go, Clemmie. Love you.'

'Love you too. Call me if you need me.'

Good news, good news—she couldn't wait to tell Luke. As she'd suspected, he had the very wrong end of the stick.

Jess flexed her hands on the wheel and eased up on the accelerator. As eager as she was to get home, she couldn't risk speeding along these windy roads, slick with incessant rain. The skies had opened up just as she'd left Lambert's Bay and the rain had followed her all the way to Paarl, and it obviously had no intention of stopping any time soon.

Jess drove her SUV through St Sylve's imposing gates and noticed that a dark green Mercedes Benz was parked outside Luke's front door. She wrinkled her nose. Luke had said that he'd be in meetings most of the day, and she hoped that his appointments hadn't run over and that he'd be finished at a reasonable time.

She had plans for him this evening...

Jess grabbed the envelope and CD that lay on the passenger seat, tucked them into the folds of the newspaper she'd bought earlier and, deciding that her bag and files could wait, ducked out of the car and sprinted as best she could in her high-heeled boots. The door opened as she grabbed the handle and she stumbled into Luke's hard chest.

'Jess!'

Jess dropped the newspaper and on a laugh flung her arms around his neck and planted her mouth on his. 'Oh, it's so good to see you. I've missed you so much.'

He grinned down at her. 'I saw you this morning, but that is nice to hear.'

Jess laughed into his bemused face, then caught a movement on the stairs. Her blood turned to ice as she saw Kelly drifting down the stairs, barefoot and wearing only Luke's favourite rugby jersey—*her* favourite rugby jersey. Jess dropped her hands and stepped back. Kelly's hair was tangled and her make-up was smudged. It didn't take a rocket scientist to work out that at some point in the afternoon Luke had removed Kelly's clothes. As for anything more than that—

she couldn't go there... Jess felt as if someone had shoved a red-hot poker in her stomach.

Luke followed her horrified stare and his muttered oath barely penetrated the roaring in her head. 'You've got to be kidding me!'

Then the red mist cleared from her mind and she shook her head. *This is Luke,* she told herself, *the man who says he doesn't cheat, ever.* He wouldn't do that to her. She trusted him.

Seeing Luke's thunderous glare, directed right at her, she knew she had to rescue the situation as quickly as she could. So she took a step forward and met Kelly at the bottom of the stairs.

'Hi—it's Kelly, isn't it? Did you get caught in the storm?'

Kelly, who'd been looking rather nervous, sent her a smile. 'I did. I was here to buy some wine. Luke, Owen and I were walking back from the cellar and we got caught in the rain.'

'Hey, Jess!'

Owen's voice drifted from the lounge and Jess briefly closed her eyes. Thank God she'd hadn't gone nuts and accused Luke of cheating...

'Luke lent me a pair of your running shorts. I hope you don't mind.' Kelly lifted up the edge of the rugby shirt and Jess saw her own shorts.

She told Kelly she didn't mind at all and watched as Kelly walked back into the lounge.

Jess started to follow her, but Luke's hand on her arm kept her in place. 'You thought that I slept with Kelly,' he hissed.

She thought about denying it but Luke would see right through her. She met his hard eyes and sighed. He was ticked...and he had a right to be. An apology was needed. Why did she keep putting herself in these positions?

She held up her hands. 'Habit reaction...' His expression didn't change and she sighed. 'Come on, Luke. I reacted, I realised I was wrong and then I tried to correct it. I'm sorry I doubted you but it really was for only a second.'

Luke narrowed his eyes at her. 'Don't do it again.'

Oh, well, this *wasn't* the way she'd thought this evening was going to go. Jess sent him an uncertain look before realising that she still had the envelope in her hands. 'Listen, I have news!'

Luke lifted his eyebrows. 'You look like you've had an interesting day.'

'I've had a great day,' Jess said as they walked into the lounge. 'I spent the day with Sbu. We finished the edit on the last advert.'

Luke frowned. 'What advert? I thought there wasn't anything you could use from the last shoot.'

'There wasn't, but I came up with something else.' Jess pulled the disc from inside the newspaper and waved it. 'Do you want to see it?'

Luke shrugged. 'Sure. What's in the envelope?'

Jess looked over at Owen and Kelly and thought that it wasn't something she wanted to discuss with an audience.

'I'll tell you later.' Jess walked over to the DVD player and inserted the disc. Flipping on the plasma screen, Jess walked back to stand next to Luke. 'I think you'll like this.'

He loved it.

He hated it.

He looked happy, he thought, jamming his hands into the pockets of his jeans, and he had been. It had been one of the nicest, most relaxed afternoons he could ever remember. The entire weekend had been a revelation; he'd laughed and kicked back, swallowed up by the warmth of the Sherwood clan. He wished that he could bank on the fact that there would be more of that type of family weekend, but that brought him back to the issue of permanence and commitment.

He'd noticed Jess and Clem filming that afternoon and into the evening, had thought it was just a video for the family archives. Jess had turned the footage into something special: gorgeous people in a gorgeous setting. It was an inspired move, Luke thought.

On film, Jess had captured all his hopes and dreams. There was John's son, Kelby, filthy dirty from digging up worms in an empty flowerbed, and Clem, lying back on her elbows, relaxed and gorgeous in the late-afternoon sun. Him and her brothers, sitting on the lawn, trading insults and getting to know each other.

Then the last frames of the film appeared on screen. Someone had picked up the video camera and filmed Jess walking towards him on the lawn, wrapping her arms around his neck and boosting herself up his body to laugh down into his face. Love and delight radiated from her. Everything she felt about him was written on her face. She was in love with him.

He didn't need her to tell him. It was there on the screen in front of him. Luke held his throat as he felt it tighten. He hadn't wanted this—hadn't asked for it. He didn't know what to do with this knowledge, her love, where to put it, how to act.

'So, what do you think?'

Luke eventually realised that Jess was talking to him and couldn't find the words he wanted to say. He didn't *know* what he wanted to say.

'Luke, do you like it?' Jess asked again, and he heard her insecure laugh. 'I kind of need an answer or else we go back to square one.'

'I think it's wonderful,' Kelly said with a quaver in her voice.

'Superb, Jess,' Owen agreed.

Luke licked his lips and looked from Jess to the TV screen and back again. 'I'll think about it. I've got to go.'

Luke hurried out of the room and pounded up the stairs to his room. Dragging off his damp jersey—he hadn't had time to change between Jess's arrival and getting Kelly sorted out with dry clothes—he shucked his wet boots and jeans and changed into a pair of track pants and a sweatshirt.

Warmer, he sat down on his bed and looked at his hands. He had to decide what he was going to do about Jess. The campaign was complete and she needed to get back to Sandton—to her business, her family, her life. Leaving him alone at St Sylve.

He didn't think he could bear it. He didn't want to be alone, but how could he ask her to stay? He wanted her at St Sylve, wanted to see her face first thing in the morning and last thing at night. But he had no right to ask her to give up her life, her business, her home, when he wasn't prepared to take their relationship any further.

He was terrified of marriage. It felt as if a noose was tightening around his neck every time he even considered the concept. Jess couldn't—shouldn't—give up her life for anything less than a solid, watertight commitment.

Six weeks ago he'd had a peaceful life: a mutually satisfying sexual relationship with a nice woman, good friends for company, work to keep him busy. A normal, busy life without a complicated woman in his bed—in his head. He'd come to terms with his childhood, made peace with his failed marriage, put his relationship with his father into perspective.

Then Jess had skidded back into his life and spun it upside down.

Sex was no longer just about sex. He'd lost his family but he'd been slapped in the face with hers. He was about to have his longest dream aired on national TV. And she was in love with him. He hadn't asked for this—any of it. Why did he have to deal with all this? It was…overwhelming, distracting, too damn much!

He felt as if he'd fallen into a vortex of information and was being sucked down...sucked dry.

'Luke?'

Luke looked up and saw Jess in the doorway, her hand resting on the doorframe. *God, what now?* Could he not just have five damned minutes on his own?

'Can I come in?'

It irritated him that she felt the need to ask. This had been as much her room as his over the past week. He nodded and she walked over to him, that yellow envelope still in her hand. She sat down next to him and he could see the shimmer of raindrops in her hair.

'I'm sorry you didn't like the advert.'

Honesty forced him to answer truthfully. 'I loved the advert. It was just a...surprise.'

Jess shoved a shaky hand into her hair and tapped the envelope on her knee. 'I brought you a present. I hope you like it.'

Luke took the envelope off her lap, lifted the flap and pulled out a wad of papers. Placing them on the bed next to him, he flipped through the documents and quickly realised that the papers related to his mother and his childhood. His past... Jess had been delving into it. A core-deep slow burn started in his stomach and an icy hand clutched his heart. She had no right to interfere.

That's not true. He heard the small voice in the back of his head. *You're angry and miserable and maybe looking for a fight. Looking for an excuse to push her out of your head. In the space of an hour she's pushed every button you have...*

'Your mother didn't leave you. She was coming back for you—'

'Shut up!'

Luke jumped to his feet and looked down at her with furious eyes. Forget maybe—he *definitely* wanted a fight. *He knew what buttons to push too.* 'You really do have a habit of thinking that you know it all, Jess.'

The colour leached from Jess's face and she stared back at him, her eyes enormous in her face. She looked at the papers on the bed, sucked in a breath and tried for a normal voice. 'You don't understand! Luke, it's not what you think. It's *good* news!'

'I don't care! What did I say when you suggested that I contact my aunt?'

'That you didn't want to do it,' Jess replied in a small voice.

'What part of that sentence didn't you understand? How *dare* you take the decision to investigate my past out of my hands? If I wanted to know I am quite capable of finding out myself!'

'I'm sorry. I thought I was doing a nice thing!' Jess protested. 'I thought you needed to know—that I was helping.'

'You know, the first time I met you I thought you were an arrogant, snotty witch. Essentially, nothing has changed.'

When shocked hurt ran across her face he knew he had scored a direct hit, but she recovered quickly.

'That wasn't what you were thinking every time you took me to bed.'

'Hey, your body was on offer. I'm a man. I just took what was available.'

'That's an awful thing to say.'

It was, but he didn't care. Somewhere in a place that was beyond his temper and his anger and his fear, Luke realised that he was hurting her—that every word that dropped from his lips was like acid hitting her soul. He didn't mean it, but he was bone-deep terrified of the implications contained in that envelope—knew that they would change his perceptions about the past, change *him*. He didn't want to deal with any of it. Not with Jess's love, with the anger he felt that his mother had died, leaving him with his monster father, with knowing how much he'd needed her in his life. He just wanted to lash out...to put all this turbulent emotion somewhere else... on someone else.

Jess had a massive target on her forehead. It wasn't noble, and it wasn't nice, but *she* was somewhere to put this burning, churning rage that had his heart, stomach and throat in an unbreakable grip.

Jess wrapped her arms around her middle. Fine tremors passed through her body—a combination of cold and emotion. She felt annihilated and utterly lost... Who *was* this man who was doing his best to hurt her? This wasn't the Luke she'd thought she knew, the man she'd come to love. He was cold, hard, ugly.

'Why are you doing this?'

'Doing what? Being honest?'

Jess took a step forward and slapped her hand on his chest. 'Don't you dare! Don't you *dare* call this being honest! This is you being a chicken-crap coward! This is you being scared of being close to someone, of exploring your feelings, of admitting that I mean more to you than a quick fling.'

Luke scowled at her. 'Get real. This is about you making decisions on my behalf, insinuating yourself into my bed and my life—'

'Insinuating myself into your bed and your life?' The words roared out of Jess with the force of a freight train. 'Who was the one who kept saying that this was a bad idea, that we shouldn't sleep together because it would get complicated? That was *me*!'

'Well, we did, and I knew that I'd regret it!'

Luke's eyes were a deep green and as hard as granite. He was slipping further and further away from her to a place where she wouldn't be able to reach him.

'Luke, please don't do this…' Jess's anger faded and she put her hand out to him. She winced when Luke jerked away from her touch. He was gone, slipped over. She'd lost him…

Jess felt her heart crack. 'Why are you deliberately mis-construing my actions?' she demanded. 'I tried to give you a heads-up eight years ago about St Sylve and you tore me apart. I believe that you need to know that your mum loved you—adored you—but I'm being told that I'm an overbear-ing, interfering, controlling witch.'

Jess heard her voice grow stronger and she squared her shoulders and looked Luke in the eye.

'And the icing on the cake? You slept with me because I was *handy*? Nice, Luke.' Jess scrubbed her hands over her face. This day had gone to hell in a handbag… Her voice vi-brated with emotion when she spoke again. 'I thought you were *it*, Luke.'

'It?'

'The person I wanted to be with for the rest of my life. It just goes to show how utterly stupid I can be on occasion.' Jess's voice broke. 'But you know what? I deserve more and I definitely deserve better. There were kinder ways to get rid of me, Luke.'

She took her keys out of her back pocket and played with them, fighting back tears. She looked around the room.

'Please ask Angel to pack up my stuff. I'll pay her to do it. I'll send a courier company to pick it up. I can't be here another second. Consider me history, Luke.'

When she was at the door she thought she heard him say her name, softly and laced with pain. But when she turned around Luke was still sitting on the edge of his bed, staring down at the carpet between his legs. It was just her active imagination, conjuring up scenes and possibilities that were impossible.

Walking away from him, from the place—the person—she considered her home took more courage than she'd known she had.

It was two-forty a.m. and Luke couldn't sleep. Instead he lay on the leather couch in front of his flat-screen, watching the final advert for St Sylve for the... He'd forgotten how many times he'd watched it. He watched Jess jump into his arms, felt his heart clench each time she did it.

The rain hammered down outside, as it had done for the past week. He'd spent the day placing sandbags next to the stream that ran past the eastern vineyard. The stream was pumping, and more rain upstream would cause it to break its banks and flood the vineyard. He recalled his grandfather talking about that same stream bursting its banks in fifty-eight and washing away a good portion of the vines.

He had no problem learning from his forefathers' mistakes.

It was learning from his own that he was having problems with.

Earlier tonight, unable to sleep, he'd reopened the envelope Jess had left behind and properly read the papers inside. The contents of which he was still trying to process...

According to the notes Jess had jotted down, his aunt had died shortly after his father passed away, but her daughter, who now lived in the cottage, had kept her mother's papers and knew about Katelyn.

Long story short: his mum hadn't left him. According to the daughter, his mother had left him at St Sylve for a couple of days while she sorted out a house to rent close to her sister. She'd already moved the bulk of his toys and clothes and his father had known that she was leaving.

He'd been an *oops*—a very welcome mistake for his mother, a way to be trapped into marriage for his father. They'd married, and the relationship had always been stormy.

His father's affairs and his inability to share his time, his money and St Sylve with her had led to her decision to leave.

She'd been on her way to collect him when she'd died. Subsequently his father had refused his aunt permission to see him or to have anything to do with him. She'd sent letters and birthday presents every year. When Luke had left school his aunt's health had been failing and she'd decided to let fate run its course. If he chose to seek her out then so be it.

He might have decided to track her down...if he'd known about her. Naturally he'd never seen the letters or the presents. How typical of his father, he thought. He hadn't wanted his mother, but her leaving St Sylve should have been on *his* terms, not hers, and he'd been left with a reminder that she'd left without permission: Luke himself.

Luke tucked a pillow behind his head. He now realised—could finally accept—that Jess had done this for *him*. She knew that there was a festering ulcer buried deep in his heart. She'd lanced it by tracking down his cousin—had started the process of healing by bringing him these papers. She knew it was necessary for him and also knew that he probably wouldn't have done it without her pushing.

The folder of papers she'd left signified a particular type of freedom: the knowledge that he'd been wanted—loved. If he'd left with his mother he wouldn't have had the material benefits his father had given him...but he would have been happier. Settled, not so neurotic about relationships.

Thanks, Dad.

Some time earlier, while reading the papers, he'd finally admitted that he was utterly in love with Jess.

Quickly following that thought had come acceptance that he *was* a 'chicken-crap coward'—that he'd been scared of loving Jess in case he lost her, terrified of facing and dealing with the pain...and guess what? He *had* lost her. She was gone.

He missed her...and he felt sick every time he remembered

that she wasn't part of his life any more. Life together. It was what he wanted. She was the other chamber of his heart— the reason the sun came up in the morning. He could see her ripe with life, carrying his child. She would be the most fantastic mother—the glue that would hold his family together. He felt settled with her—calm, in control. Nothing much was wrong with his world if he could see her smile first thing in the morning.

He finally understood what love felt like...*Jess.*

Just Jess.

They were meant to be together; they would be together. He just had to find a way to make that happen.

Logistically, it was a nightmare. Her home, her life, was in Sandton. His was here at St Sylve. How much could he give up for her and, more importantly, would she even have him?

If he had to he would leave St Sylve. It would be a wrench, but if there was a choice between St Sylve and Jess, being with Jess would win. St Sylve was his heritage but Jess was his soul.

Luke rolled over, pointed the remote and switched the TV off. As soon as it was light he'd head for the airport, catch the first plane he could find and go to Jess.

He'd go to her because wherever she was, simply, was where he wanted—needed—to be.

Jess paced her mother's kitchen, a glass of red wine in her hand, her thoughts a million miles away. Her father sat at the kitchen table, sketching, and her mother was making an apple crumble that Jess knew, from thirty-odd years of eating her mother's food, would taste like cardboard.

When she refused to eat some she would only be telling the truth when she explained that along with destroying her heart Luke had also taken her appetite.

Clem stood at the stove, and Nick was somewhere in the

house fixing something. He and Clem were in town for a couple of days to give Clem her 'city fix'. It amused Jess that Clem's need for a city fix always seemed to coincide with something that needed to be done at her parents' house. It was, Jess knew, Clem's very clever way of re-establishing and cementing Nick's relationship with his parents after years of little or no communication.

Clem walked over to her and put her hand on her shoulder. 'Oh, Jess, I *do* know what you're going through. The month I spent without Nick was the loneliest, hardest of my life.'

Jess rested her head on Clem's shoulder, dry-eyed but exhausted. 'It's been a week and my heart is shutting down...I never knew it could hurt this much.'

'I have to tell you that your brothers are making plans to go down there and beat the snot out of him,' Clem informed her. 'There have been mutters about broken knees and cracked heads.'

Jess looked horrified. 'They can't! Honestly, why can't they mind their own business?'

'Because you *are* our business, Jessica Claire,' her father said, his eyes focused on his sketch. 'But I have faith in that young man. He just needs to get his head around the fact that he's loved and in love.'

'You don't know Luke, Dad. He's stubborn...'

'But I know young men. I raised four and I was young myself once. Every one of your brothers took some time to shake off their...*ahem*...attachment to their bachelor lifestyle, to their freedom. I did the same.'

'David cried and squealed like a girl when I told him I wouldn't put up with him seeing other girls and that getting stoned regularly was not an option,' Liza informed them crisply.

Her comment made Clem laugh, and Jess just managed a smile. She pulled out a chair and slumped into it. She wished she could tell them Luke's reluctance to get involved wasn't a normal man's fear of commitment, that it was rooted in his childhood, in his mother's death, his father's lack of love.

Jess looked up at Clem. 'You were right, Clem. Heck, *he* was right... I shouldn't have interfered.'

Clem shrugged. 'He'll come to realise that you did it out of love and he'll forgive you.'

'I doubt it,' Jess replied.

David looked up from his sketch of Clem. 'Did his cousin say anything about Katelyn's paintings?'

'Apparently they are all in the attic at her cottage. Janet didn't realise that Katelyn was such an important artist.'

'Is she going to sell them?' Liza asked.

'No, she said they are Luke's, and she'll leave them where they are until he decides what to do with them. If he decides to do anything with them,' Jess muttered darkly. 'The list of paintings was in the envelope with the rest of the documents.'

'I'd love to see them,' David said reverentially.

Jess picked up a fork and traced patterns in the bright tablecloth with its tines. 'You and me both. But there is no chance of that, Dad.'

'Keep the faith, darling.' David patted her hand. 'And if nothing happens with Luke, just remember that your mother has the numbers of at least three young men who'd like to meet you.'

Jess couldn't smile at his joke. She doubted she'd ever date again. That was the trouble with meeting your soul mate— it was difficult to imagine, comprehend being with another man. Even if said soul mate wanted nothing to do with her.

Liza saw something in her face that made her step forward and run a hand over her head. 'Forget your brothers. I have a good mind to beat him up myself.'

Jess looked up into her mum's sympathetic face. 'It just hurts so much, Mum.'

Liza wrapped her arms around Jess's neck and Jess rested her cheek on her stomach. 'I know, baby girl. I know it does.'

Later on that afternoon, not knowing that he'd missed Jess by a couple of minutes, Luke stood at her parents' front door and met Nick's cold grey eyes. He thought that the possibility of Nick's fist rocketing into his jaw was quite high. Jess's brother scowled at him, and the muscles in his forearms bulged when he folded his arms and widened his stance. Luke thought he could take him, if he had to, but if Nick punched him he wouldn't retaliate. He deserved the punch and more.

'You have five seconds to state your case before I rip your head off,' Nick snarled, his grey eyes thunderous.

Luke thought fast and decided to keep it simple. 'I love her and I want to marry her.'

Nick stared at him and Luke braced himself. Nobody was more surprised when Nick's face cleared, his arms dropped and a huge smile split his face. 'Cool. C'mon in. Jess isn't here, though.'

Luke stayed where he was. 'You're not going to hit me?'

Nick looked amused. 'Do you want me to?'

'No, I'll pass. But...why not?'

Nick swung the front door open. 'You took nearly a week to realise that you are an idiot. I took a month. The point is you got there, and you are doing something about it. You *are* doing something about it?' he asked.

'Of course I am,' Luke replied irritably.

'Then why are you here and not at her place, grovelling?'

'I'm not quite ready to see Jess yet. Well, I am—but there's something I have to do first and I need help.'

Nick clapped a hand on his shoulder. 'I'm your man. I can't wait to watch the merry dance my sister leads you for the rest of your life, mate.'

As long as she's dancing with me, I don't give a damn,

Luke thought. 'I need you and at least one other of your brothers to help me transport something...'

Jess was at home and wishing she could stop waiting for Luke to call. She propped her feet up on the coffee table and sighed. She had a huge, Luke-sized hole in her life and a smaller St Sylve hole next to it. She kept telling herself that life had a funny way of sorting itself out, but the words weren't sinking in. She had loved and lost. Millions had, and it wasn't the end of the world...it just felt like it.

Jess sat up, hearing a key in her front door lock, and turned around to see the door opening. 'For crying in a bucket, Patrick! Hold it up!'

She heard another couple of muffled swear words from... *Nick*? Looking towards the front door, she saw three pairs of feet: trainers, loafers and—oh, God—scuffed work boots. And three pairs of legs behind a massive brown-paper-wrapped frame.

Jess stood up, her hand to her heart as the frame wobbled and Luke cursed. 'Damn! Be careful. Okay, lower it against the couch. Slowly... This was not the greatest idea I've ever had.'

Jess had no words so she just stared at them, watching as Nick glared at Luke across the top of the painting. 'I said that, Sherlock.'

Patrick straightened and theatrically placed his hand on his back. 'Gee, I thought I mentioned it too. But, no, you had to make the grand gesture.'

Luke grinned at them. 'You sound like a bunch of groaning grannies. For two sports freaks, you two could moan for Africa.'

Nick glared at him. 'Bite me.'

Luke was here—finally here. His back was to her and she sucked him in. His hair was almost ludicrously long, curling over his collar and falling into his eyes. The long sleeves of his T-shirt were pushed up over his elbows and he wore his oldest, most faded and frayed jeans. Three-day-old stubble completed his surfer-boy look.

Jess's mouth watered.

Then her heart hardened as she remembered that he thought she was an overbearing control freak, an interfering witch. And how dared her brothers use the key she'd given them for emergencies to saunter into her house without so much as a hello or any type of greeting?

She was sick of arrogant, egotistical, selfish men!

'You have thirty seconds to leave my house before I start going bananas,' Jess told them, her voice hard and cold. She waved at the brown parcel—obviously a painting. 'And take that with you. I have nothing to say to you, Savage.'

'Well, I've got a couple of things to say to you,' Luke replied in a mild voice as his eyes flicked over hers, softened and bounced back to her brothers. 'Okay, you two can leave now.'

Nick and Patrick exchanged a long, considering look and Patrick shook his head. 'Forget it… I want to know why you chartered a plane to deliver that painting and why we had to babysit it like our firstborn in a truck over here. Are *you* going anywhere, Nick?'

Nick folded his arms. 'Heck, no! Clem would kill me if I didn't get every romantic moment. Get on with it, Luke, you're wasting time.'

'Like I'm *really* going to have this conversation in front of you two,' Luke scoffed.

'Nobody is having a conversation with anybody!' Jess stormed to the door and gestured for them to get out. 'You're all leaving—now!'

Luke looked at her brothers. 'C'mon, guys, give me a

break. I need to talk to Jess and you're not helping. Just go! Please?'

Nick placed his hands together in an attitude of prayer and bowed low. Patrick followed suit. 'May the force be with you,' Nick intoned.

The brothers bowed again before backing out through the front door and slamming it behind them.

Luke said something uncomplimentary about them under his breath before he raised his head to look at Jess. 'Hi.'

Jess shoved her shaking hands into the front pockets of her jeans. 'What are you doing here, Luke? I thought you said everything of importance a week ago.'

'Not quite.' Luke looked around her small house. 'Nice place.'

Jess shrugged and sent a curious look towards the painting—it could *only* be a painting—then gestured to the kitchen. She had no idea why Luke was delivering a painting to her house after a week of silence and her pride refused to allow her to ask. 'Do you want something to drink?' she asked in a polite, cool voice.

Luke nodded and followed her into the sunny kitchen. Jess handed him a bottle of beer and they took up their customary positions of leaning against opposite counters. They spent a couple of minutes just looking at each other.

Luke eventually broke their hungry silence. 'You look good.'

Jess lifted her eyebrows. He was either using flattery or her looks hadn't gone to pot yet. 'You look tired.'

Luke picked at the label on his beer bottle. 'Listening to those two bitch for hours will do that to a man.' Rolling a tiny ball of paper between his fingers, he flicked it towards the dustbin.

'I'm surprised to see you and my brothers on such good terms,' Jess said, annoyed. Where was her siblings' outrage on her behalf? The desire to beat him up—metaphorically, of course. She didn't want him actually hurt—because he'd broken her heart? Traitors, every last one of them.

'Well, I practised my grovelling on them before coming here.'

'Is that what you've come to do? Grovel?'

'If I have to.' Luke placed his untouched bottle of beer on the counter and rubbed his hand over his jaw. 'I hope it won't come to that. I have a great deal to say to you and I hope you'll hear me out.'

'You're here, in my kitchen, and I can't kick you out or gag you, so I don't have much of a choice, do I?' Jess retorted.

It was so unfair that he could look so good and she couldn't touch him. That he was so close and yet still so inaccessible. She couldn't read his eyes, couldn't find a clue to what he wanted to say in his inscrutable face, his tense body.

'Thank you for finding out what happened to my mother.'

'Even though I interfered and took the decision out of your hands?' Jess asked, sceptical.

Luke shoved his hands into the back pockets of his jeans and rocked on his heels. 'I was scared to do it—scared of what I'd find out. I had finally come to terms with my mother's death and I didn't want to have to live with something else. When you handed me that envelope I felt like you were pushing me somewhere I didn't want to go.'

Jess grimaced at the reluctant note she heard in his voice. 'You're still not happy I did it.'

'I've been on my own for so long that I find it difficult to accept help—to feel comfortable with someone...'

'Meddling? Interfering? Snooping?'

'Concerned about me,' Luke said firmly. 'It'll take some getting used to.'

Jess felt her heart roll over in her chest but dismissed the spurt of hope as her imagination. 'That implies that there will be a tomorrow for us?'

'I'm hoping that there will be a lifetime of tomorrows.'

Jess licked her lips. 'You called me a control freak and overbearing, said you understood why my exes kicked me into touch. Snotty and interfering…'

'I know, I know…I'm sorry. But I'd been slapped with a whole lot of things that day that I didn't know how to deal with and I was reeling. You were in the splash zone.'

'Like what?' Jess demanded.

'When you—briefly I'll admit—thought that I'd slept with Kelly, I was hurt. I wanted you to trust me implicitly, but you hesitated.'

'I did trust you—when I started thinking and not reacting.'

'Then I saw the ad, saw all my dreams captured on screen, and I felt at sea. And then I realised that you loved me…'

'Not any more,' Jess stated, her colour heightened.

'Liar,' Luke countered. 'I realised that you loved me but I didn't know what to do about it. How could I ask you to leave your family, your business, your life to live with me? Someone who has no idea how to be part of a family, who doesn't know how to give you what you need? Then you hit me with my past and it was too much…it was all too much. I miss you, Jess. I need you in my life.'

'You hurt me,' Jess said in a small voice. 'You took my heart out and stomped on it. And now you're back, asking me to risk it again?'

'I want to be with you, Jess. I want you to be my family.'

Luke rubbed his shoulder with his hand. Jess heard his expulsion of air.

'After my anger subsided and I looked at the folder I needed some time to think it all through: my mum, my father, you.'

'And?'

'And I'm glad to know that my mum loved me. I realise

that my childhood is over and, most important, that I want to be with you—make a commitment to you. I don't do that lightly or easily, because when I do, I do it with everything I have.' Luke stepped forward and placed his hands on either side of Jess's hips, effectively blocking her in. 'I'm so in love with you.'

Jess gnawed on her bottom lip and looked up at Luke with wide, scared eyes. 'So what are you suggesting, Luke, exactly?'

'I realise that you can't leave your business, so can we find a compromise? You spend a week with me at St Sylve, then I spend the next week with you here?'

When Jess didn't answer, Luke sped up. 'If that doesn't work for you I'll leave St Sylve, let Owen run it. Hire a vintner...go back to venture capital full-time.'

'You'd hate it,' Jess pointed out.

'But I'd be with you, which is the most important thing to me.' Luke raised an enquiring eyebrow at her still-troubled face. 'What's the problem, Jess?'

As Luke turned those amazing eyes to hers she stepped away and paced to the fridge and back, wringing her hands. 'Look, Luke, you say you love me now, but I don't know if you are going to change your mind again. I don't know if I can run that risk. I don't know if my...' She stuttered to a stop and then forced the words out. 'If my heart can stand it.'

Luke looked at her, his face expressionless. Then, taking her hand, he yanked her towards the lounge and made her stand in front of the wrapped painting. He looked at her, a small smile on his face. 'Somehow I knew that I would need a grand gesture.'

Jess was utterly bemused as Luke went to stand at the side of the package. Bunching the paper at the corner edge with his fist, he looked at Jess, his heart in his eyes. 'This is my most prized possession—possibly the only material thing I'd try to rescue from a fire. And you fell in love with it a couple of weeks ago.'

Luke ripped the paper and revealed the enormous paint-ing that graced the large space above his bed at St Sylve. The mountains jumped out at her and the mist glistened. Jess wanted to climb into the painting with Luke and make love between the vines.

Ignoring her galloping heart, she forced a shrug. 'I don't understand.'

Luke patted the frame. 'This is, apart from you, my great-est treasure. If there was one thing I'd risk my life to save it would be this. I just want to know if I can share it with you.'

'But why? Are you giving it to me? You can't give it to me!' Jess squeaked. 'It's one of only two paintings you have of your mother's.'

Luke half smiled. 'I can, because the same thing that calls to me in this painting calls to me in you. Your strength, your generosity, your utter courage and your bloody stubborn-ness. And because I love you. You've got to know how much I love you.'

Jess couldn't help her knees buckling. She sat down on the edge of the couch and stared up at Luke, absolutely baffled. She felt Luke's arm around her shoulder and instinctively dropped her face into his neck, winding her arms around his head in case he disappeared as quickly as he'd appeared.

Luke ran his hand over her hair. 'Sweetheart, are you cry-ing? Because if you are Nick will beat me to a pulp. Not that I don't deserve it, but I'd rather avoid it if I can.'

Jess lifted her head and her eyes were clear, bright and happy. She hiccupped a laugh. 'Do you mean it?'

'Which part? The loving you or the Nick beating me to a pulp?' Luke teased.

Jess slapped his chest and placed her thumb between her teeth. 'Luke?'

Luke kissed her hair. 'I love you, Jess, with everything in me. I think I probably fell in love with you eight years ago and never really stopped. I'm sorry I hurt you. Let me share your life, Jess. In Sandton, if you want to stay here, or at St Sylve.'

Biting her bottom lip, Jess stared at the painting and back at Luke, who suddenly didn't look as confident as he usually did. Maybe she hadn't loved and lost as she'd first thought.

Forcing her bubbling laughter away, Jess pursed her lips. 'My decision rests on a couple of assurances from you.'

'As much wine as you can drink, I'll replace any thong I rip with two more, and my house and land and my heart are in your hands.'

'Shut up,' Jess ordered, her mouth twitching. 'I want a child. Or two. Maybe three.'

'Sold,' Luke responded quickly, joy flooding his face. 'What else?'

'I want to go home—back to St Sylve—and I want the painting to go back into our bedroom. And I want you to marry me. So if you don't think that might happen some time in the future maybe you should walk away now.'

Taking her chin, he lifted her face to look up into his. 'I was made to love you, to look after you, to protect you, to make beautiful, beautiful babies with you. Will you marry me?'

Jess's mouth fell open. 'You're proposing? Right now?'

'That's what "will you marry me?" means. Feel free to say yes any time.'

His eyes held an element of doubt and she reached up to touch his jaw with her fingertips. 'I'll marry you because my sun rises with you, because I want to carry your beautiful, beautiful babies, because I want to tell you every day that nobody will ever love you as much I do and will.'

Luke rested his forehead against hers. 'Oh, Jess, you take my breath away. I don't have a ring for you yet. I was focused on getting you back and hadn't dared hope that you might consider marrying me. Maybe we could have one designed?'

Jess sent him a look long of adoration. 'Just knowing that I'm going to spend the rest of my life with you is enough.'

Luke cupped her face in his hands. 'I love you so much.'

He kissed her thoroughly, reverentially, and Jess fell into his embrace, happiness seeping out of every pore. Her hands were undoing his shirt buttons when his mobile rang.

Luke cursed, yanked it out of his pocket and looked down at the screen. He turned the screen to show Jess. 'Nick, your nosy brother.'

Jess pressed a kiss to his chest. 'Ignore him.'

Luke dropped the phone, but it had barely hit the cushions when it rang again. Two seconds later Jess's mobile started to chirp in the kitchen.

Jess dropped her head back and hissed her frustration. 'They'll keep calling until they know what's going on.' Jess reached for Luke's phone and put it to her ear.

'Can I not just be amazingly happy for five minutes without you guys wanting in on the action?' Jess demanded, her hand on Luke's cheek. She smiled as Nick spoke, said goodbye and then sent Luke a bemused look.

'Nick says that you're not to forget about the silky bantams. Um…why do you need to buy some chickens?'

Luke just laughed and kissed her.

EPILOGUE

SIX WEEKS LATER Jess's family swept in *en masse* to an exhibition of Katelyn Kirby's paintings. They were surrounded by an amazing collection that had the art world buzzing—but what was the first thing her mother said on seeing her?

'He still hasn't put a ring on your finger!'

Jess rolled her eyes and pulled her left hand out from her mother's grasp. 'Mum! Luke and I are getting married in six months' time. An engagement ring is not going to change that.'

'Every girl should have a ring!' Liza stated.

'And I'll get one…when Luke finds exactly what he is looking for,' Jess told her, and turned to greet the rest of her extensive family. 'You're late. Luke is about to do his speech.' Jess snagged her father's jacket and pulled him back. 'Dad, you can view the art later…come here.'

Clem made her way to stand next to her and slipped an arm around her waist. 'It's good to see you so happy, Jess. You *are* happy?'

'Absolutely.'

'And how are you coping with your business?' Clem asked, taking a glass of champagne from a hovering waiter.

'Ally has picked up the reins and is not letting go. I have very little to do with the Sandton office except for designing the initial concepts.'

'And the Cape Town office?' Nick asked from his position behind Clem.

Jess looked rueful. 'I haven't set it up yet, and I don't know if I'm going to. I've been doing a bit of consulting here and there, looking after clients in the city.'

Clem lowered her voice. 'And St Sylve? Is it on a bit more of an even keel?'

Jess looked past Clem's shoulder at Luke. 'There's been a pick-up in sales and that's encouraging. I'm also renovating the manor house to turn it into a venue suitable for small weddings, functions...family weekends away, so I'm swamped. Happily, crazily busy. We're designing a house that we want to build on the other side of the farm, and...'

'And Luke keeps you busy...?' Nick added dryly.

Jess fluffed her hair and grinned. 'He most certainly does—and in the most delightful ways possible.'

Nick scowled. *'Blergh.'*

Jess laughed and stood in the middle of the half-circle her family made. She watched Luke, looking tall and strong and amazingly attractive in his black tuxedo, step up to the podium. She felt the glow in her stomach when he looked for her, and his eyes were warm and loving when they connected with hers. They were wildly in love and amazingly happy. Jess, ring or not, considered herself a very lucky woman.

Luke looked around the room and smiled. 'Welcome to this exhibition of Katelyn Kirby's art—my mother's art. As most of you know, she died when I was really young, but this huge collection of her work has recently come to light and I wanted to share her talent with the world. Some of the paintings here are not for sale—my fiancée, Jess, and I have decided to keep some—but the rest of her art, including her sketches for jewellery designs and sculptures, are being sold to raise money for a foundation we've established in her name to fund the training of talented, disadvantaged young artists.'

A few minutes later Jess watched as Luke walked towards her, with that slow, sexy smile on his face. He greeted her family before dropping a sexy kiss on her mouth. His green eyes sparkled as he looked down at her.

'I have a present for you,' he said.

Jess did a little dance in her ice-pick heels. 'You do? Will I like it?'

'I hope so. It has the added benefit of getting your mum to stop nagging you—and me.' Luke sent Liza a full, teasing look and grinned widely when she wrinkled her nose at him. Turning back to Jess, he pulled out a box from his pocket and flipped open the lid.

Jess stared down at the soft, romantic, deeply unusual ring. It was unique—swirls of gold and platinum, with a deep sapphire winking up at her.

Luke's voice was laced with emotion when he slipped it on to her finger. 'My mum designed it, and when I saw her sketch I thought of you—thought that she'd drawn it with you in mind. I snuck it out of her portfolio before you could see it so that it would be a surprise. What do you think?'

Jess bit her lip in an effort to hold back her tears. 'I love it. I love *you*.'

Luke cupped her face with his big hands. 'Love you more.'

Nick broke the emotionally charged moment. 'Jeez, Savage, if you're going to get soppy you'll end up being our least-favourite brother-in-law,' he drawled. 'It puts far too much pressure on the rest of us to be romantic.'

Luke grinned at Nick, Jess plastered to his side. 'I'll be your *only* brother-in-law,' he pointed out.

Nick pulled a face, laughter in his eyes. '*You're it?* Then I definitely need another large drink!'

* * * * *

Mills & Boon® Hardback

May 2013

ROMANCE

A Rich Man's Whim	Lynne Graham
A Price Worth Paying?	Trish Morey
A Touch of Notoriety	Carole Mortimer
The Secret Casella Baby	Cathy Williams
Maid for Montero	Kim Lawrence
Captive in his Castle	Chantelle Shaw
Heir to a Dark Inheritance	Maisey Yates
A Legacy of Secrets	Carol Marinelli
Her Deal with the Devil	Nicola Marsh
One More Sleepless Night	Lucy King
A Father for Her Triplets	Susan Meier
The Matchmaker's Happy Ending	Shirley Jump
Second Chance with the Rebel	Cara Colter
First Comes Baby...	Michelle Douglas
Anything but Vanilla...	Liz Fielding
It was Only a Kiss	Joss Wood
Return of the Rebel Doctor	Joanna Neil
One Baby Step at a Time	Meredith Webber

MEDICAL

NYC Angels: Flirting with Danger	Tina Beckett
NYC Angels: Tempting Nurse Scarlet	Wendy S. Marcus
One Life Changing Moment	Lucy Clark
P.S. You're a Daddy!	Dianne Drake

Mills & Boon® Large Print

May 2013

ROMANCE

Beholden to the Throne	Carol Marinelli
The Petrelli Heir	Kim Lawrence
Her Little White Lie	Maisey Yates
Her Shameful Secret	Susanna Carr
The Incorrigible Playboy	Emma Darcy
No Longer Forbidden?	Dani Collins
The Enigmatic Greek	Catherine George
The Heir's Proposal	Raye Morgan
The Soldier's Sweetheart	Soraya Lane
The Billionaire's Fair Lady	Barbara Wallace
A Bride for the Maverick Millionaire	Marion Lennox

HISTORICAL

Some Like to Shock	Carole Mortimer
Forbidden Jewel of India	Louise Allen
The Caged Countess	Joanna Fulford
Captive of the Border Lord	Blythe Gifford
Behind the Rake's Wicked Wager	Sarah Mallory

MEDICAL

Maybe This Christmas…?	Alison Roberts
A Doctor, A Fling & A Wedding Ring	Fiona McArthur
Dr Chandler's Sleeping Beauty	Melanie Milburne
Her Christmas Eve Diamond	Scarlet Wilson
Newborn Baby For Christmas	Fiona Lowe
The War Hero's Locked-Away Heart	Louisa George

Mills & Boon® Hardback
June 2013

ROMANCE

The Sheikh's Prize	Lynne Graham
Forgiven but not Forgotten?	Abby Green
His Final Bargain	Melanie Milburne
A Throne for the Taking	Kate Walker
Diamond in the Desert	Susan Stephens
A Greek Escape	Elizabeth Power
Princess in the Iron Mask	Victoria Parker
An Invitation to Sin	Sarah Morgan
Too Close for Comfort	Heidi Rice
The Right Mr Wrong	Natalie Anderson
The Making of a Princess	Teresa Carpenter
Marriage for Her Baby	Raye Morgan
The Man Behind the Pinstripes	Melissa McClone
Falling for the Rebel Falcon	Lucy Gordon
Secrets & Saris	Shoma Narayanan
The First Crush Is the Deepest	Nina Harrington
One Night She Would Never Forget	Amy Andrews
When the Cameras Stop Rolling...	Connie Cox

MEDICAL

NYC Angels: Making the Surgeon Smile	Lynne Marshall
NYC Angels: An Explosive Reunion	Alison Roberts
The Secret in His Heart	Caroline Anderson
The ER's Newest Dad	Janice Lynn

Mills & Boon® *Large Print*
June 2013

ROMANCE

Sold to the Enemy	Sarah Morgan
Uncovering the Silveri Secret	Melanie Milburne
Bartering Her Innocence	Trish Morey
Dealing Her Final Card	Jennie Lucas
In the Heat of the Spotlight	Kate Hewitt
No More Sweet Surrender	Caitlin Crews
Pride After Her Fall	Lucy Ellis
Her Rocky Mountain Protector	Patricia Thayer
The Billionaire's Baby SOS	Susan Meier
Baby out of the Blue	Rebecca Winters
Ballroom to Bride and Groom	Kate Hardy

HISTORICAL

Never Trust a Rake	Annie Burrows
Dicing with the Dangerous Lord	Margaret McPhee
Haunted by the Earl's Touch	Ann Lethbridge
The Last de Burgh	Deborah Simmons
A Daring Liaison	Gail Ranstrom

MEDICAL

From Christmas to Eternity	Caroline Anderson
Her Little Spanish Secret	Laura Iding
Christmas with Dr Delicious	Sue MacKay
One Night That Changed Everything	Tina Beckett
Christmas Where She Belongs	Meredith Webber
His Bride in Paradise	Joanna Neil